BE... ®

MINNIE'S MISSION OF MAXIMUM MISCHIEF!

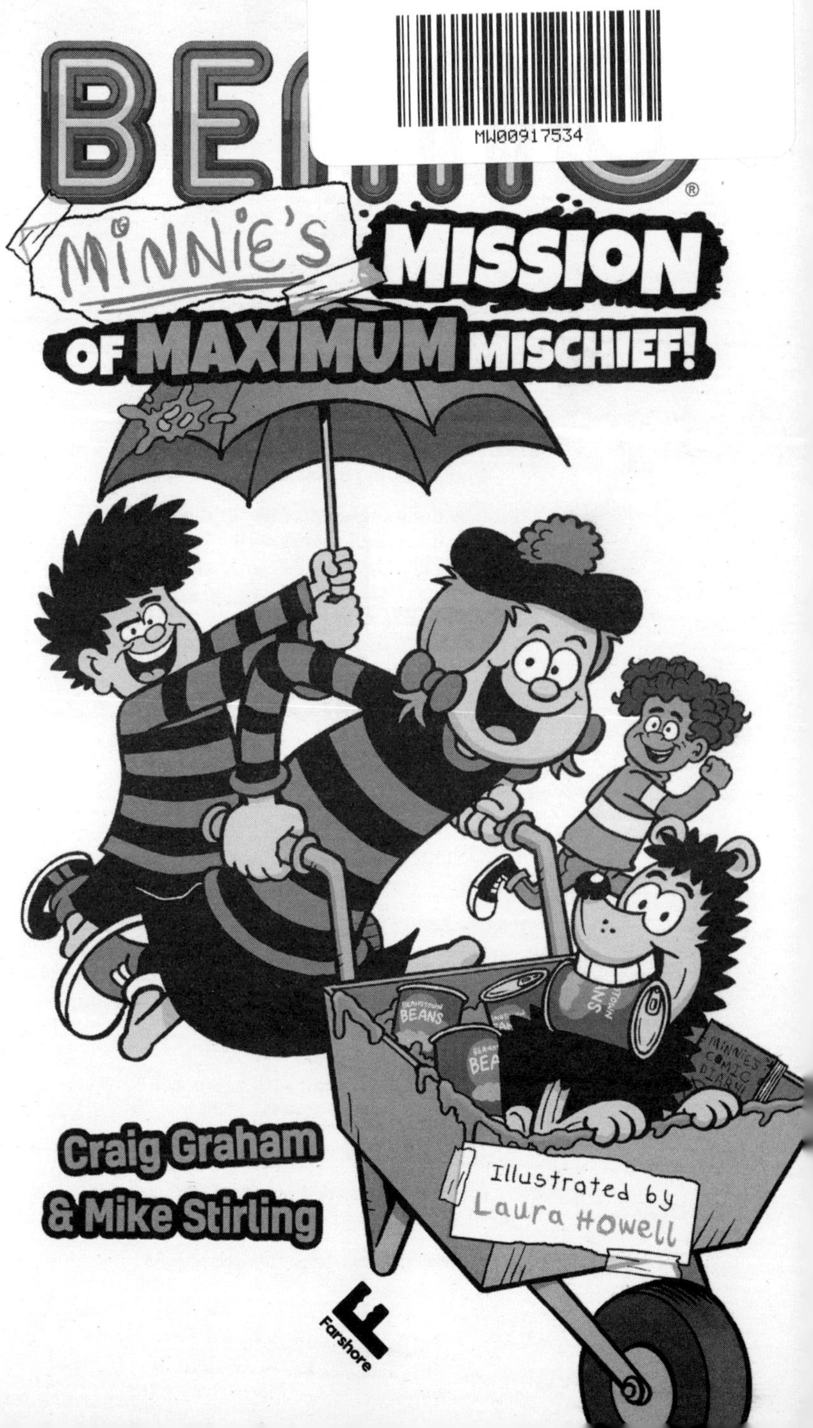
BEANS
Illustrated by
Laura Howell

Craig Graham
& Mike Stirling

Farshore

First published in Great Britain 2023 by Farshore
An imprint of HarperCollins*Publishers*
1 London Bridge Street, London, SE1 9GF
www.farshore.co.uk

HarperCollins*Publishers*
Macken House, 39/40 Mayor Street Upper,
Dublin 1, D01 C9W8, Ireland

Written by Craig Graham & Mike Stirling
Illustrated by Laura Howell
Additional Illustration – Ed Stockham
Creative Services Manager – Rhiannon Tate
Executive Producer – Rob Glenny
Text design by Janene Spencer

BEANO.COM

A Beano Studios Product © DC Thomson Ltd (2023)

ISBN 978 0 00 860397 7
Printed in Great Britain
001

Contents

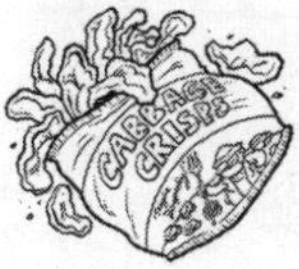
CABBAGE CRISPS

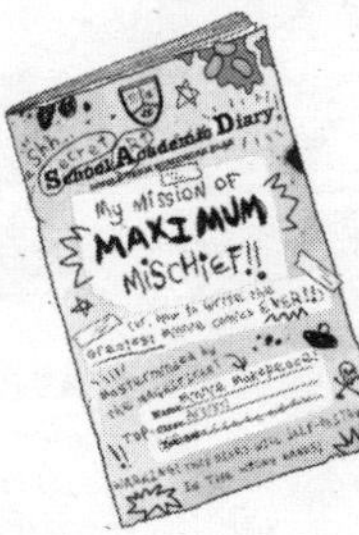
Diary
My MISSION OF
MAXIMUM
MISCHIEF!!

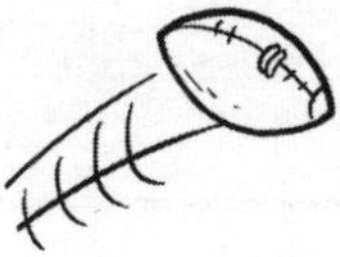

MEET TEAM MINNIE!

If you're reading Minnie's **FIRST** *boomic*, here are the ace faces you're about to become besties with!

'Book' + 'comic', geddit?

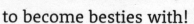
MINNIE
THE STAR OF THE STORY! FLICK TO THE BACK OF HER BOOK TO MAKE YOUR OWN COMIC DIARY!

DENNIS
MINNIE'S COUSIN & BEANOTOWN'S PRANKMASTER GENERAL!

GNASHER
DENNIS'S BEST BUDDY HAS JAWS THAT CAN CRUMBLE CONCRETE!

HARSHA CHANDRA
HARSHA'S JUST AS GOOD AT PRANKS AS DENNIS, AND HER DAD OWNS BEANOTOWN'S BEST JOKE SHOP!

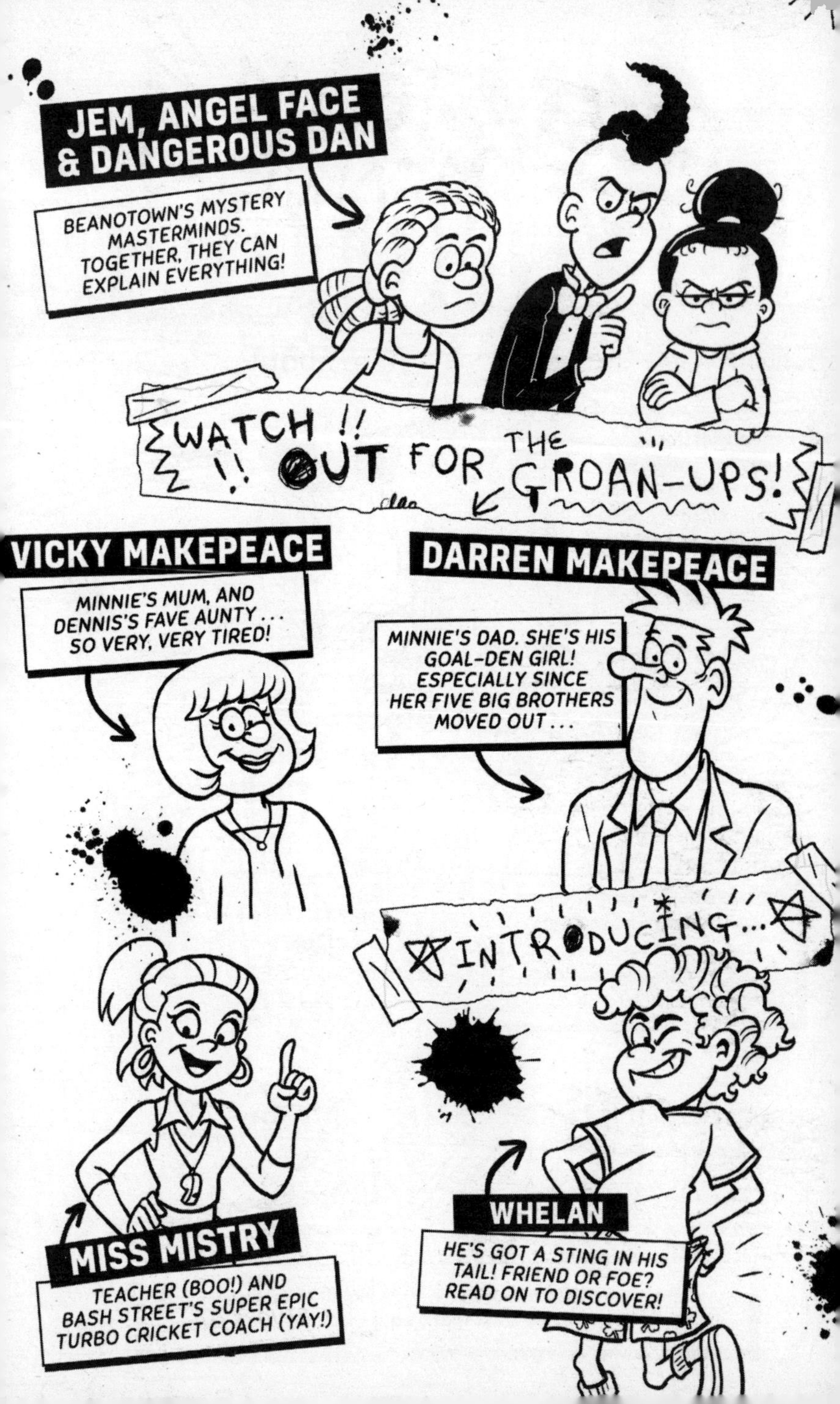
JEM, ANGEL FACE & DANGEROUS DAN
BEANOTOWN'S MYSTERY MASTERMINDS. TOGETHER, THEY CAN EXPLAIN EVERYTHING!
WATCH OUT FOR THE GROAN-UPS!
VICKY MAKEPEACE
MINNIE'S MUM, AND DENNIS'S FAVE AUNTY . . . SO VERY, VERY TIRED!
DARREN MAKEPEACE
MINNIE'S DAD. SHE'S HIS GOAL-DEN GIRL! ESPECIALLY SINCE HER FIVE BIG BROTHERS MOVED OUT . . .
INTRODUCING...
MISS MISTRY
TEACHER (BOO!) AND BASH STREET'S SUPER EPIC TURBO CRICKET COACH (YAY!)
WHELAN
HE'S GOT A STING IN HIS TAIL! FRIEND OR FOE? READ ON TO DISCOVER!

Welcome to... BEANOTOWN!

Beanotown Library. Some say it's Beanotown's tallest building – it has the most stories, you see!

The Makepeace family live here. Minnie's five older brothers have moved out, meaning peace and quiet for her long-suffering parents (as if)!

This is where the Menace family lives. Menaces by name, menaces by nature. At least that's what the neighbours say!

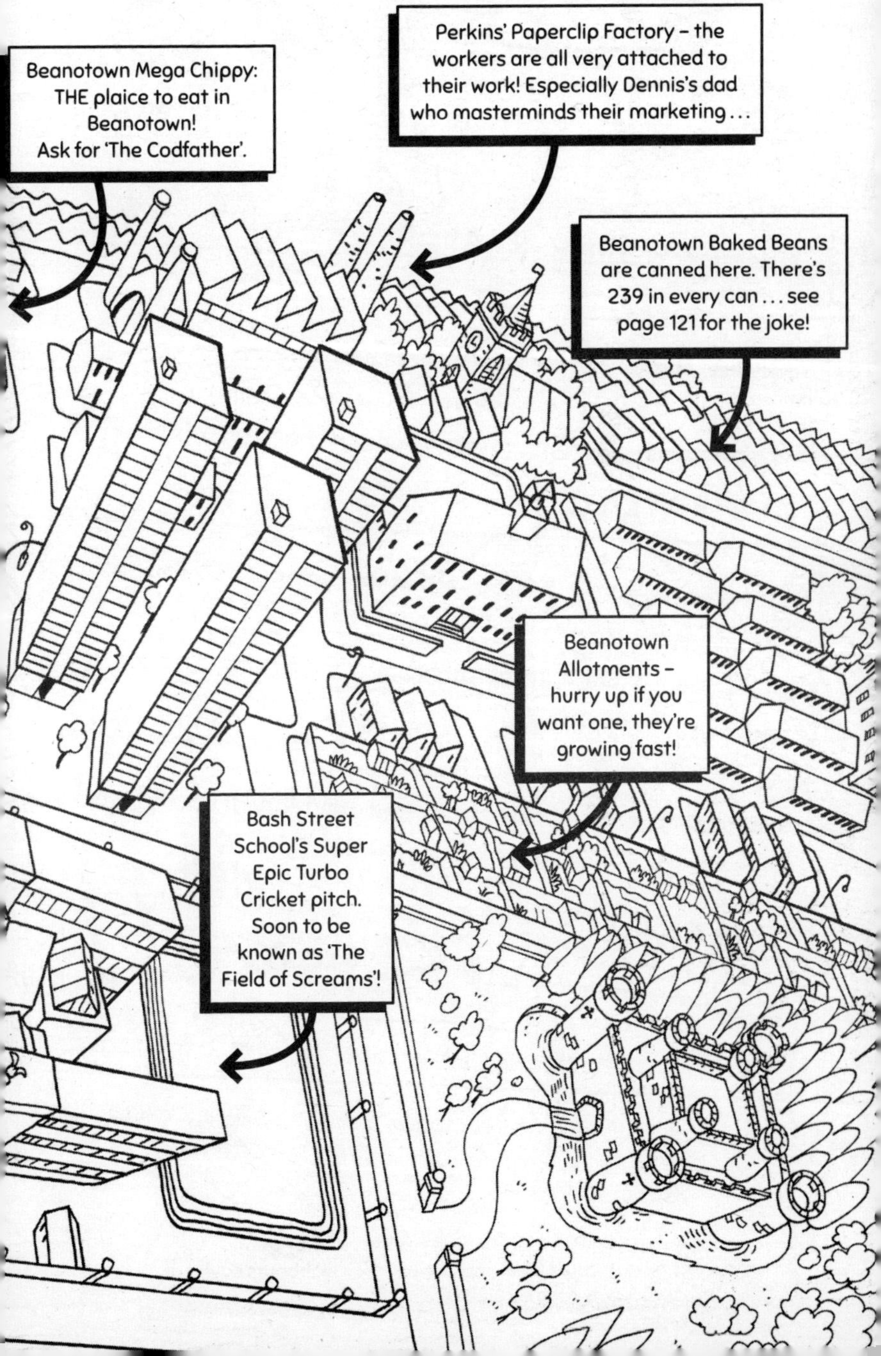

Beanotown Mega Chippy: THE plaice to eat in Beanotown! Ask for 'The Codfather'.
Perkins' Paperclip Factory – the workers are all very attached to their work! Especially Dennis's dad who masterminds their marketing . . .
Beanotown Baked Beans are canned here. There's 239 in every can . . . see page 121 for the joke!
Beanotown Allotments – hurry up if you want one, they're growing fast!
Bash Street School's Super Epic Turbo Cricket pitch. Soon to be known as 'The Field of Screams'!

Gasworks Road, Beanotown
Today (is gonna be MY day)

Dear AWESOME READER!

You expected another boomic about Dennis, huh?
Good news! This story is going to be about
someone far more awesome, witty, smart,
talented, cooler-looking and interesting
than him: ME!

I know, I know. I'm so ~~generous~~ generous. You can
thank me later.

I've taken part in other Boomics before, but
this is the one where I TAKE OVER!

I feel the need — the need to read!
Let's get this party started.

MINNIE MAKEPEACE!!

P.S. I've snuck in some of my own secret diary pages,
to make this a bit more ME!

Chapter One

MINNIE OF THE MATCH

WOOFT! It was the best of goals; it was the worst of goals.

An amazing scorpion kick. Sensational. The type of goal Hermione 'Minnie' Makepeace had always dreamed of scoring.

Except, she hadn't scored it. A loudspeaker confirmed the worst.

'LEGWEE DRIBBLERS 1, BASH STREET NIBBLERS* 1 – and what a STRIKE from Legwee's team captain, Whelan! GAME ON! Legwee's Ready to RUUUUMBLE!' shouted a Legwee student commentator.

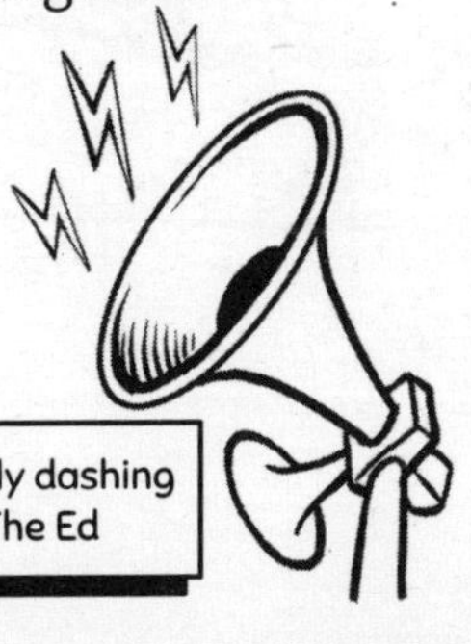

*A nickname awarded due to Gnasher's habit of illegally dashing onto the field and 'gnipping' opponent's shorts! – The Ed

It was the quarter final of the Super Epic Turbo Cricket European Tour of Mischief, versus the Legwee Academy Dribblers, in County Cavan, Ireland.

Icy rain fell – thick, mean and heavy – and Minnie had faceplanted in the mud trying to stop the scorer.

'Stinking butt-warts,' she cursed.

At least she'd missed his celebration, where he'd skidded on his knees towards a gaggle of adoring fans standing underneath a banner dedicated to him.

'Whelan' looked like he belonged in a boy band: golden brown skin and dark curls, which bounced as he ran.

'C'mon, Minnie, get off your butt. We need to hit back, **NOW!**' yelled Dennis. He'd scored the opening goal and was annoyed they were level.

Her cousin tried to haul her up, but she shrugged him off so quickly he slipped and plopped into the mud bath beside her.

'Easy, Cuz – save that for the opposition!' he smirked.

Dennis was team captain. That miffed Minnie. She knew she was the better player. Dennis just had the knack of always being in the right place at the right time . . . to steal the glory!

But not today. Nope. This was her moment to shine.

Minnie knew her entire family back home were watching on a You-Hoo livestream. She imagined her five older brothers laughing at the state she was in.

None of them had ever won this tournament and Mum had promised this was her chance to shut them up. But so far, things weren't going to plan.

It was March 17th, St Patrick's Day, a national holiday in Ireland. Minnie had never played in front of such a noisy crowd before.

PWEEEEEP!

The half-time whistle was blown by Miss Mistry, Minnie's coach. One of the quirks of Super Epic Turbo Cricket was that the team playing away from home provided the referee.

'Give us a penalty in the second half, please?' begged Dennis.

Unfortunately for them, Miss Mistry was too fair for that, which was a bit of a pain today. But no one complained. She was an ex-Bash Street Kid herself, so when she spoke, the team listened.

She explained the opposition was a one-star team. They just needed to pull together to win. They just needed to pass more and work together. 'Teamwork makes the dreamwork.'

Minnie gazed at the ground. She knew she was the main target for that message.

'Did you hear that at home? With just a bit

of teamwork, Bash Street has this game in the bag!' Stevie Star said into his microphone.

He was enthusiastically presenting a livestream for those back home in Beanotown. Stevie loved making videos. He was excited as he knew the whole town was watching.

He was interrupted by his co-presenter, Harsha Chandra, Beanotown's most precocious prankster!

'Today is Dennis's 10th birthday. Can he celebrate by saving his team, after his cousin's epic fail?!' she asked.

'We'll see,' laughed Stevie. 'Super Epic Turbo Cricket is the greatest sport in the universe.'

'We'd maybe even think about playing it ourselves, if it wasn't so ridiculously dangerous,' she kidded herself.

'In case they've been living under a rock, let's remind the fans at home why Super Epic Turbo Cricket is so awesome. Here's something we made earlier,' said Harsha as a video explaining the history and rules of the game started.

Harsha: Super Epic Turbo Cricket was invented in 1938 by Pansy Potter, a former Bash Street Kid, and it is one of the best pranks to ever be played on teachers in Bash Street's history. Why?

Because it's not cricket at all – she just told the teachers that, so that they'd think it was a civilised sport and say yes to them playing it! She's our hero.

Stevie: The first rule is to break as many rules as possible. The pitch is a footy pitch, with the same goals and nets, but the ball is oval-shaped.

Harsha: Players can kick, throw, or hold onto the ball, but must bounce it every three steps. This stops the 'belly ball' dodge, where players stuff the ball up their shirt and run straight into the goal.

Stevie: It's a game of two halves, twenty-five mins each, with no injury time. Which is lucky, cos slide tackles, rugby tackles, body checks and kung-fu kicks are all encouraged. Watch out!

Harsha: You can kit yourself out with equipment from any other sport. Hockey or hurling sticks, baseball bats, golf clubs, tennis and badminton racquets. Anything goes. But you're only allowed to hit the ball with them, not opposition players or teammates. Lassos and tripwires are banned. For now.

Stevie interrupted. 'The teams are back out for the second half. Twenty-five minutes until triumph or disaster.'

Bash Street School were less than three matches away from becoming champions for the first time ever. And Minnie wasn't about to mess that up.

Minnie intercepted a pass that was intended for Whelan.

'**Gotcha!** That's what I call Min-tutition!'

She'd sussed the Dribbler's game plan: to set up Whelan for a scorpion kick at every opportunity. Mistry had been right all along.

'MINNIEEEEEEEEEEEE!'

Minnie heard her cousin's scream. Dennis had an open goal on the other side of the penalty area.

'No way, cuzzy wuzzy. This one's mine.'

There was no chance she was passing. This was her chance to prove that she was every bit as good as any boy – and one boy in particular. She was going to perform the perfect scorpion kick. She bounced the ball ready to strike. Her foot flashed towards it, and . . .

. . . she missed completely! Minnie's boot bashed into her nose, knocking her back into the mud. The crowd roared with laughter.

When someone kicks themselves in the face, it's traditional for their Numskulls to abandon ship . . . –The Ed

As she toppled, a pair of hands nabbed the ball. It was Whelan – who else?

He shimmied past Jem and bounced the ball as he closed in upon on Rubi in goal.

Dennis tried to distract Whelan.

'There's a lion on the pitch chasing you!'

'**Argh!** It's been eaten by a shark!'

'**Whoa!** A T. rex has grabbed the shark!'

The only danger for Whelan was that he pulled a muscle giggling. A T. rex couldn't grab a shark with those funny little arms.

He wound up to clinch the match!

Just then, from out of nowhere, a furry blur bowled Whelan over.

'STRIKE!' yelled Dennis, laughing as Whelan hit the deck.

Whelan was skittled. He'd lost his chance of glory, had two grazed knees PLUS a MAHŌŌSIVE gaping hole in his shorts!

'Butt-tastic! I knew you were pants,' mocked Dennis, as Whelan frantically tried to cover his embarrassment.

The blur had been Gnasher! Dennis's Abyssinian wire-haired tripe hound had taken direct action to clear the danger.

The crowd gasped. Then an angry chant started up.

'Who let the dog out? Who? **Boo! BOO! BOO!!'**

This wasn't covered in the Super Epic Turbo Cricket rulebook. Miss Mistry looked utterly bemused. She had to make a call.

'Rules are highly overrated,' offered Dennis.

Miss Mistry fumbled in her pocket, then raised a RED CARD!

Dennis sniggered. She'd ordered Gnasher off. Result! He hadn't even been on the team to start with.

Then it dawned slowly on him that
Miss Mistry was pointing at him!

'Worst! Ref! Ever! You've just lost us
the match,' he spluttered. But there was no
changing her mind. Gnasher was his dog,
so was his responsibility.

RED CARDS ARE WORSE THAN REPORT CARDS...

He trudged off miserably. Gnasher was
waiting apologetically behind the goals, the

match ball clamped – burst and deflated – in his jaws.

'Disaster for Dennis. That's another fine mess Minnie has gotten him into! Bang go Bash Street's chances,' shrieked Harsha. She had a fair point. If Minnie had passed, none of this might have happened.

'It's the first time in the sport's history that a player's been sent off!' said Stevie. 'Miss Mistry looks devastated.'

'It's not all bad,' chuckled Harsha. 'There's no way Legwee's star player can continue after such a terrible injury . . . to his shorts.'

But, as she laughed, one of Whelan's adoring fans threw him some fresh shorts, which landed on his head. They were vomit-orange, with green shamrocks woven into them with itchy-looking wool.

Best of all, across the butt, embroidered in bright-pink lettering, it said 'Sweet Cheeks'.

But Whelan pulled them on and blew a kiss towards his saviour. He winked at Minnie. The cheek!

Miss Mistry just shook her head. If Minnie had only listened and passed to her teammate, they could've been in the lead with a full team ready to see the game out.

Instead, she'd had to award Legwee a dreaded 'penalty flick'.

It allowed the opposition to flick mud, bogies and bubblegum to distract the goalie, while the fouled player aimed a free shot!

Rubi Von Screwtop twirled on the middle of her goal line. Partly to dodge the boogers, partly to put Whelan off. You couldn't scorpion kick a penalty, so she had a chance. A tiny chance.

'Here comes Whelan, the star of the match,' said Stevie. 'He shoots! It's a . . . '

'MISS!' yelled Harsha.

But Harsha was talking about Miss Mistry, who she'd spotted sneakily pointing to where Whelan was aiming, to help Rubi make the save! Well I never!

It worked! Rubi deflected the ball towards Minnie, who raced towards her shot at glory. Whelan zoomed after her, like a shark chasing a jet skier!

'Pass!' yelled Dennis, from the side-lines. 'GNASH!' barked Gnasher. Surely Minnie wouldn't mess up again?

Whelan heard the bark and was reminded of how he'd been cheated. He launched himself into a vicious slide tackle.

The last thing Minnie heard, before being hacked, was Miss Mistry shouting, 'Remember, make the dream work, Min!'

For the first time ever, Minnie listened to a teacher. She passed the ball to James, who tripped over it and tumbled head over heels, tangling himself into the back of the net.

Well, reader, can you spot the ball? – The Ed

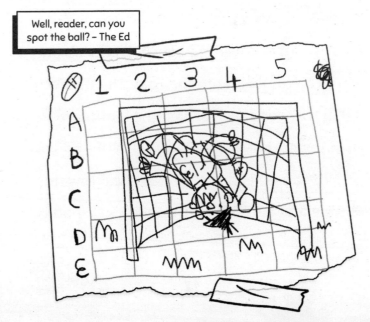

Minnie was dazed. Whelan was frantically apologising. She shushed him and asked what everyone was thinking . . .

'Where's the ball?'

There was an eery silence, as if both sides were too scared to imagine their best and worst fears coming true.

Harsha spotted the reality first and shared the answer:

'IT'S IN THE NET! BASH STREET WINS!'

The ball had wedged between James's knees before he tumbled into the goal. The unluckiest kid in the world, had scored the jammiest winning goal of all-time.

Whelan extended a muddy hand towards Minnie and smiled. 'It's St. Paddy's Day and

he's discovered the luck of the Irish. You
deserve it.'

APART FROM WHEN I LOOK IN THE MIRROR, YOU'RE THE BEST PLAYER I'VE SEEN TODAY!

The final whistle blasted!

Calamity James was carried off shoulder
high by his teammates (falling twice in the
process) but it was Minnie who was awarded
player of the match.

Dennis spotted Miss Mistry comforting
Whelan, of all people.

'Hang on . . . she's hugging him!
BIZARRE!'

Minnie shook her head, 'I'll *never*
understand teachers.'

The inspirational, wise and extremely
mischievous Miss Mistry spotted them staring.
She was unfazed. 'You made our dream work,
Minnie – Bash Street's in the semi-final!'

Chapter Two

SHE SMELLS SEASICK, BY THE SEASHORE...

Minnie and her teammates were still buzzing as they boarded the ferry home. Miss Mistry could barely make herself heard above the constant babble.

'**DENNIS!**' she yelled.

Everyone turned towards her instantly, to see what trouble he was in now. So did Dennis, as he was sitting quietly.

Miss Mistry smiled with satisfaction. 'Now I have your attention, Mrs Creecher has just WotSlapped me. You can pick anything you want to eat from the boat's canteen. Dinner's on her!'

A massive whoop went up! This was an unexpected bonus. It was most unlike the head teacher to hand out treats.

'Gut-bustin' boat burgers and ice cream floats all-round!' yelled Jem as she high-fived Rubi in celebration. The kids queued and were soon ordering one of everything available.

WARNING: Only to be enjoyed occasionally as part of balanced diet ... and never, EVER on a boat ... – The Ed

Soon after, the sea sickness started. Waves of it. Dinner was on everyone now.

It was like a gross domino effect. Calamity James was the first.

The sight and smell triggered the rest of the team.

PHOOEY! BLEURGH!
PHOOEY! BLURP!
PHOOEY! BARF!

Minnie and Dennis sat together, unaffected, at the other side of the canteen. They'd stuffed chips up their nostrils, dodging the nasty niff.

I MOUSTACHE YOU A QUESTION, MIN!

They spoke in that stuffy voice you get when your nose is blocked.

Ed's tip: Read out this loud while holding your nose to get the full effect!

'Who's this Huey, everyone keeps asking for?' joked Minnie.

'Dunno, but he's pals with RALPH!' laughed Dennis. 'I thought it was only me who got an early BARF today!'

Minnie wiped her saucy fingers, plucked a pencil from behind her ear and started sketching in a scruffy notebook.

'What's that? Homework!' It looked like Dennis was about to puke too.

'As if!' replied Minnie. She paused, pondering whether she wished to confess her secret hobby. 'It's my comic diary. I've been drawing one for years.'

'Eh, I didn't know you wanted to be an artist?' said Dennis.

'I don't. I just find it . . . I dunno . . . relaxing, I guess,' replied Minnie.

'I used to keep a diary too. Well, a prank journal,' Dennis admitted. 'But my parents found it and claimed it was a confession of all the times I'd pranked them. I may as well have crossed out "diary" and written "EVIDENCE" on the front.'

Minnie laughed. 'Mine's got some wiggle room. It's not completely realistic. But it helps me look back and work things out. Sometimes, I just draw things the way I wish they could've been.'

'It's still risky, Min. Give it to me; I'll chuck it safely overboard.'

Instead, she spun the book around to show Dennis what she'd been drawing.

It was Minnie executing a perfect scorpion kick, with Whelan holding up one of those stupid fan banners, except instead of 'I heart Whelan', this one said 'I wish I was Minnie'.

'**Whoah**! You've got a crush on him,' teased Dennis.

'No, I **CRUSHED** him!'

'Liar! Liar! Bum's on fire.'

Minnie hated it when Dennis said that.

It was so stupid. Especially since he'd just finished a Mount Beano Volcanic-Butt Silly-Chilli Burger. If anyone's bum was about to reach melting point, it was his!

Minnie couldn't understand why the girls supporting Legwee went so wild about Whelan. He was good-looking. No-one could deny that. But there was something about him that bugged her.

The way he sucked up to Miss Mistry after the game was icky. As cool as she might be, she was still a teacher at the end of the day. Gross!

To shut Dennis up, she added tusks from the corner of Whelan's mouth, a wart to his nose and switched his cheeky grin to an ugly frown. A frilly tutu with oversized clown shoes completed the edit.

Dennis found the picture hilarious.

Minnie was chuffed. 'Sometimes, the pen is mightier than the catapult.'

'Are you doing homework, Minnie?!' It was Miss Mistry, returning from dropping their classmates off at the sick bay.

Minnie considered hiding her diary from view, but what would be worse, Miss Mistry seeing her awesome comic diary or her thinking she was doing homework *willingly?!* She had a reputation to protect.

Miss Mistry was impressed by Minnie's drawings. She'd started a diary when she was ten too.

'It's a great idea,' said Miss Mistry. 'It helps you suss stuff out and learn from your mistakes. Plus, it gives you something brilliant to read on boring journeys!'

'Life looks better in funny pictures,' Minnie agreed.

'Plus it keeps you occupied and out of mischief,' Miss Mistry said affectionately.

It was true. Doodling about her day, then

talking about it with Dennis, had made time fly. They'd not pulled a single prank on the boat!

A bell rang to say they were nearly home.

'Time to lose the nostril fries, please.' Mistry passed them each a paper hanky with a wink.

Minnie breathed in the sweet smell of success. Well, sawdust and disinfectant. But things were looking up.

She was returning home as a hero! Or was she?

Chapter Three

THE MIN OF THE MOMENT KEEPS SMASHING IT!

'The most successful Makepeace of all-time is HOME!' yelled Minnie.

WHOOMPH!

She slammed the front door shut with all her force, signalling her triumphant return.

CRASH!

She cringed.

TINKLE!

She held her breath.

'HERMIONE!' yelled her parents in grumpy unison.

Minnie sighed.

They only ever used her full name when she was in trouble. What was their problem now? It was a tradition in her family to always celebrate success loudly – especially when it was your own! You had to shout out, to stand out.

Until recently, her home life had been shared with five super-successful big brothers: Michael, Martin, Morris, Mark and Max.

But over the years they'd all moved out, leaving the house a far calmer place.

As if!

Minnie was more trouble than her brothers combined, according to her parents. It was tough work being the youngest in a family of high achievers, but Minnie considered herself more than up to the task.

Down the hallway, Mum was crouched over the remnants of her favourite family portrait, Dad standing behind her, looking less than pleased.

Before she could be blamed for its destruction, Minnie bombarded her parents with details of the game.

Minnie spat them out like a rapper. She felt as if she was describing someone else, it was all so awesome! **PHHT**, who was she kidding? It all sounded exactly like her!

She waited for the celebratory hugs. But instead, Dad was still scowling. Mum had cut her finger trying to move a shard of glass from the picture frame.

Minnie tried her usual tactic. Make them laugh. 'I've invented a family jigsaw. The Make-pieces!' she giggled.

Mum and Dad looked tired and fed-up.

Mum spoke first, 'Please can you just go to your room, Minnie?'

'But Mum, I've only just got home. I have so much to tell you—'

'She said go to your room,' Dad said sternly.

Minnie winced. She felt a Minnie Meltdown building inside her. The last time she'd erupted, she screamed so loudly, a priceless Ming vase* had shattered. It had been the best way to get her parents' sympathy with five noisy big brothers. But she hadn't erupted since they'd left.

Instead of screaming, she ran to her bedroom and slammed the door as loudly as she could, satisfied when she heard another picture frame drop.

*At least that's what her dad told their insurance company. It was really from the bargain bin at Widl, Beanotown's shopping emporium. – The Ed

Chester, the family cat, scrambled off the bed and hid in her wardrobe. Animals are good at sensing bad vibes.

I NEED NINE LIVES EVERY DAY TO LIVE HERE!

Five minutes later, Minnie heard a KNOCKETY-KNOCK-KNOCK on the front door, followed by her Aunty Sandra's familiar 'Ding!'

'Dong,' her big sister, Vicky, replied, completing the traditional family greeting.

Minnie decided to risk creeping downstairs. Sandra rushed over to give her a hug.

'Well done! We were rooting for you! When Dennis got sent off, I was so embarrassed, but you saved the family honour.'

She lifted Minnie's hat
and kissed the top of her
head. Minnie felt instantly
better. Meltdown avoided.

'Have you got your stuff ready?'

'What stuff?' asked Minnie.

'For a celebratory treehouse sleepover at
our place – tonight!'

'RESULT! I'm on it!' Minnie dashed
upstairs and collected her black-and-red striped
pyjamas and a change of clothes for tomorrow.
She also grabbed her cuddly shark, Bruce. He

had real-life shark teeth sewn
into his mouth, which meant
he was risky for cuddling,
but epic in a pillow fight.

You're gonna need a
bigger bed! – The Ed

45

Snuggled up in sleeping bags in the tree house, the cousins stared out of the makeshift skylight* and up at the stars.

*Really just a hole in the roof made from the time they'd thought a giant indoor catapult was a good idea. – The Ed

They were playing their favourite game, Cosmically Rude. It was like a game of imaginary dot to dots, where they used the stars to map out the grossest things they could spot up there.

CHEEKY!

'I can just spot Uranus!' they both said at the same time. This cheered Minnie up.

A nagging thought was distracting her. Unplanned sleepovers were usually the result of a secret grown-up problem.

Work, a meeting, a hole in her bedroom ceiling – OK, that wasn't strictly a grown-up problem, as Minnie had been the one to take home the giant indoor catapult after the skylight incident.

But . . . Maybe her parents were debating sending her to Dandytown's boarding school.

Again.

Minnie started to leaf back through her comic diary, going through her recent mischief to raise her spirits. Surprisingly, it had been quite a quiet year. For her, at least. She'd put itching powder in Miss Mistry's coat, poured custard in Dad's shoes and played a prank call on Mrs Creecher. As far as she was concerned the evidence was clear.

'Your comics are epic,' laughed Dennis. 'The state of your mum and dad! My angry aunty and upset uncle. Good work, Minnie!'

He wasn't wrong. Minnie grabbed her diary back and started searching for the last time she'd drawn her parents not perma-raging.

But lately, it wasn't just Minnie they seemed annoyed with. It was each other. They argued about silly things. Dad leaving his pants on the kitchen floor, or Mum singing in the shower. Stuff they used to laugh about together, now bugged each other.

'Ta da!'

Minnie found something. She'd scribbled a comic when they'd gone to have the Makepeace Family Photo taken. The one she'd turned into a jigsaw.

The photographer, a jolly dude, had actually *told her* to make mischief.

'The family that laughs together, smiles together,' he said.

The grown-ups had overlooked the mischievous mayhem they experienced on the shoot, after they saw the results.

Minnie showed the photograph to Dennis.

'You're telling me the last time they laughed together was after you pranked them?'

Minnie nodded. A brilliant plan was forming in her mind.

'What if I pulled an epic prank on Mum and Dad? To make them laugh again. The family that laughs together . . . '

'. . . SMILES together!' replied Dennis. They high fived. Minnie started to sketch out the plan for her greatest mischief ever . . .

Chapter Four

NEW-KID CHAOS

It was 8:45 on Monday morning. School started in fifteen minutes. No time for a shower.

PLEASE TELL ME IT'S THE WEEKEND?

Minnie had slept in. Again. Neither Mum nor Dad had bothered to wake her.

Minnie pulled on her favourite black-and-red jumper. The school version, which was knitted from itchy wool.

She could hear Mum snoring.

Mum denied she snored. A recent argument started when Dad teased her about it. Minnie thought he deserved a medal for sleeping through it!

Minnie always made a packed lunch on a Monday. It was 'Cabbage Surprise Day' for school dinners.

She zoomed through the lounge into the kitchen, hurdling something mahoosive poking out from the sofa.

It was leg. A human leg.

DUN! DUN! DUN!

Don't worry reader, it's not *that* type of book! – The Ed

It belonged to her dad, who was sleeping like a baby on the sofa. He was even sucking his thumb! He had a troubled look on his face. **Weird**. Maybe he wanted a night off from the snoring symphony? Minnie snapped a sneaky selfie beside him. It could come in useful in future if he tried to embarrass her. She quickly prepared her packed lunch. A marmalade and chocolate spread wrap, was her main course. Plus some Minnie MegaMix (raisins and wasabi peas) and a tin of pop. The infamous Mad Bull Energy Drink, instead of the tiny cartons of healthier apple juice Mum preferred her to take.

She packed her trusty peashooter, carefully wrapped in a napkin to keep it secret from any snooping teachers.

Exactly fifteen minutes after waking up, Minnie hurtled through the imposing school gates. She was going to make it . . .

Minnie had been clothes lined. She sprung back to her feet, dazed and confused.

'What. Was. That?!!'

Her jaw dropped. To her utter disbelief she'd been wiped out by Whelan. Legwee's golden boy. The Scorpion Kick King. He looked flustered.

'What do you think you're doing here?' Minnie demanded.

'Sorry, I didn't see you there!' he replied. 'Here, let me help you u— Oh, it's you. Never mind.' He flashed a cheeky grin and dashed off, before Minnie could even think of a reply.

DRIIIIIIIIING

The school bell had sounded. He'd made her late!

Minnie sneaked into class. If she could just make it to her seat without Miss Mistry spotting her . . .

'Good afternoon, Minnie.' Classic teacher bants. She was barely a minute late.

'Very funny, Miss Mistry'

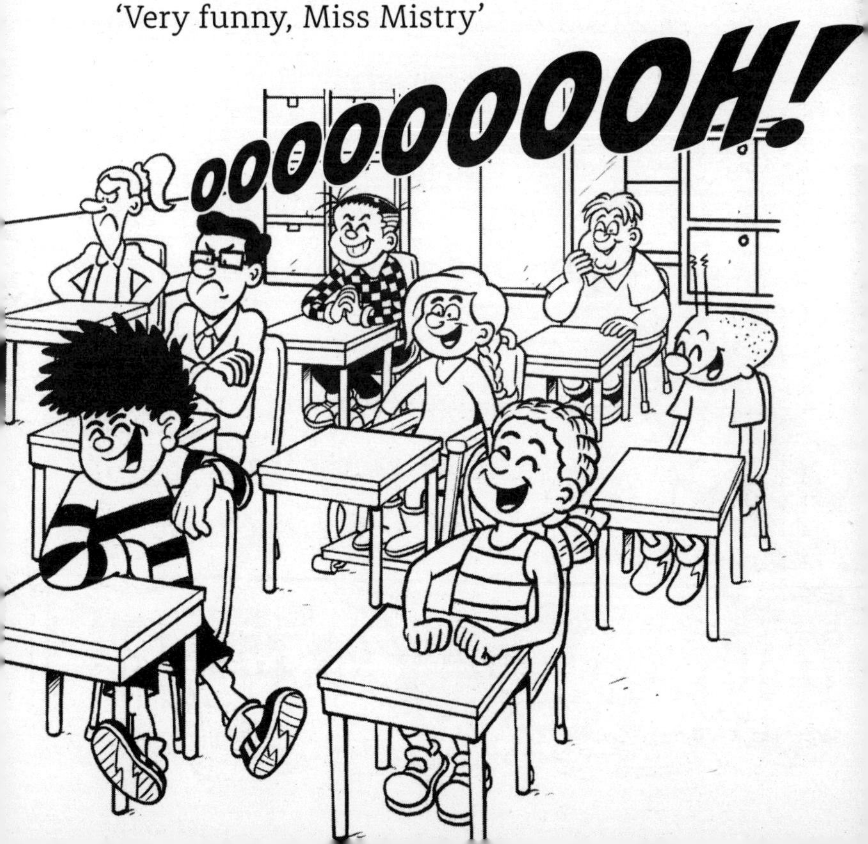
OOOOOOOOOOH!

Her classmates appreciated Minnie's come-back. Miss Mistry was not to be messed with.

'What's today's excuse then?' Miss Mistry asked. Not because Minnie was especially late – in fact, two minutes was a record for her – but because Minnie's excuses were always wild . . . and actually pretty amusing.

For once, Minnie decided to tell the truth. 'I was hacked down outside by the captain of Legwee Dribblers.'

Her classmates roared with laughter.

Outrageous! Minnie was in for it now.

Dennis piped up. 'That's a worse excuse than me saying my dog ate my homework.'

this will stop anyone copying it! Gnash if!

GNASHER

Miss Mistry simply smiled, then ordered the class to settle down.

Minnie should have been delighted, but there was something seriously sus about the way Miss Mistry hadn't accused her of making it up like the rest of the class.

She'd barely reacted when he'd been mentioned. It was like it hadn't surprised her at all. Still, her lateness had been forgotten about. **Result!**

She nudged Dennis, hard. 'Better excuse than you thought?'

Dennis rolled his eyes. Minnie was good. Even he had to admit that.

'Still have Whelan on your mind, then?' he asked with a waggle of his eyebrows.

'**Urgh, no!** It's true. He's here.'

'YEAH RIGHT!'

When the bell rang for break, Minnie made a dash for the playground. She was going to track Whelan down and show Dennis she was telling the truth.

Minnie tumbled head over heels.

Unbelievable! He'd wiped her out, for the second time that day, as he'd rushed out from Class 3A.

Dennis tripped over them both!

Miss Mistry fell over the three of them! The test papers she'd been carrying fluttered into the air.

Opportunistic pupils in the area made a grab for them and stuffed them in the bin before she could right herself.

'Told you,' Minnie said to Dennis and her teacher, as she untangled herself.

The cousins stared at Whelan, awaiting an explanation for his clumsiness.

'I was looking for the tuck shop. Someone in class warned me the school dinners are a bit dodgy.' He shot an accusatory look at Miss Mistry, who rolled her eyes.

Minnie's suspicious mind was now in overdrive. First the hugging, now the shared looks. What was going on?

'Don't spend all your money on snacks. Cabbage is good for you!' said Miss Mistry as she got up and brushed her clothes down. Whelan bolted. Again.

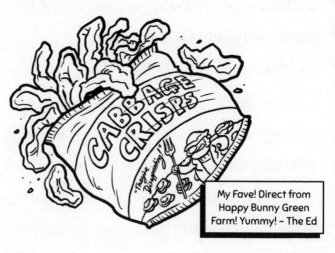

My Fave! Direct from Happy Bunny Green Farm! Yummy! – The Ed

The next period was gym, which was a shared class between 3A, 3B and 3C on the school football pitch.

While the rest of the classes played hockey, the Super Epic Turbo Cricket team were going

to practise for the semi-finals with Miss Mistry.
This was going to be epic, thought Minnie.

Unfortunately, her good mood was about
to be wrecked.

Miss Mistry asked everyone to gather
round. Whelan was beside her,
looking a little sheepish.

'I'd like you all to
welcome our new player,
Whelan,' she said.

'He can't join us!' cried
Minnie indignantly.

'He's the enemy!' added Dennis.

'I'm just a sub,' explained Whelan, whose
face had turned red with embarrassment.

Miss Mistry calmed them down.
'Remember, teamwork makes the dream work.'

Dennis continued complaining, but Minnie decided to try some trick shots. Badly. She spotted Whelan was watching her.

'You know my scorpion kick. Would you like to know the secret?' Whelan asked.

Minnie fixed him with a cold stare.

'Are you *boysplaining*?'

Whelan gulped. 'Nope. I got special training from my dad. I'm, er, just passing it on.'

Minnie folded her arms. 'Harumph. OK, Scorpion King, I'm listening.'

Whelan explained that success was all about timing. You must wait for exactly the right moment to launch your STING.

Minnie couldn't wait to unleash her new skill. Dennis had been watching and was unimpressed. He chucked a ball over and moved between the goalposts.

'There's no way you'll beat me with a handstand-heel bash.'

Whelan launched a looping pass towards Minnie. She kept her eye on the ball . . .

'Three, two, one . . . STING!'

She caught it perfectly. The ball curled towards the top corner of the goal!

But Dennis stretched out, and tipped it onto the bar . . .

'What a SAVE!' yelled Whelan.

. . . only for the ball to drop down onto his spiky head and bounce into the back of the net.

'ARRRGHHH!' yelped Dennis.

'Calm down, give me some credit for once,' said Minnie. Trust Dennis to take the attention away from her.

But she soon realised something was wrong. Whelan and Miss Mistry raced over to Dennis. As he'd fallen, his ankle had folded underneath him like a bendy straw.

It started to swell, bulging as if he'd stashed Paul the Potato down his sock.

Miss Mistry sent Calamity James to search for the school nurse, who came out to examine Dennis's ankle.

'You're lucky,' she said. 'It's just a sprain, not a break. You won't be able to run on it for two months, though.'

'Lucky?' cried Dennis. 'That means I'll miss the rest of the Super Epic Turbo Cricket European Tour of Mischief!' Dennis looked up at Miss Mistry. 'It also means we need a new captain. Fast.'

Dennis spotted her glance towards Whelan. How very dare she?

'I vote Minnie,' said Dennis LOUDLY. The team cheered in agreement.

Minnie's pride swelled quicker than her cousin's ankle had.

Miss Mistry had the last word. 'OK, that's settled. Minnie's captain and Whelan's promoted off the bench.' She confirmed her decision with a formal handshake for Minnie, then high-fived Whelan.

Dennis did a double take.

Move over Walter, Whelan was Bash Street School's newest teacher's pet.

'Come on, Dennis. Let's help you inside. You can sit on the comfy reading chair for the rest of the day,' said Miss Mistry.

'RESULT!' Dennis shouted.

Chapter Five

THE SCHOOL RUMOUR MILL!

The school canteen was even rowdier than it normally was.

As well as the usual flying food, there was a buzz in the air, and it wasn't coming from the insects hovering around the cabbage stew pot.

Everyone was discussing Whelan.

Jem, Dangerous Dan and Angel Face were the school's mystery masterminds. Minnie had called them together to suss out their new Irish teammate.

'Whelan's here to get revenge on Gnasher.'

Dennis had his ankle propped up and on ice.

He was still down in the dumps after his trip

to the sick room.

'Nothing and no one can harm Gnasher.

Especially not Whelan – I don't feel any

mean vibes,' said Jem. Dennis trusted Jem's judgement more than anyone's.

'Maybe he's an international spy, like me,' suggested Dangerous Dan, Beanotown's youthful secret agent.

'Investigating why Bash Street continually produces the world's most-well behaved pupils,' added Minnie. They all burst out laughing at that theory.

'The truth is stranger than the rumours,' said Angel Face. Minnie's ears pricked up.

Angel Face was famous for supplementing her pocket money by taking on detective work. If you wanted to find out who fancied who, or why someone was mad at you, you asked Angel Face.

She explained that Walter Brown – the mayor's son, class sneak and teacher's pet – had asked her to investigate the rumours that Whelan was Miss Mistry's new favourite pupil. Walter was worried he was losing his status as the ultimate teacher's pet.

She'd got to work straight away, investigating Whelan's social media.

'My fee was a book of Fartnite top-secret gamer cheat codes!'

'**Whoah**!' said Minnie. 'That's generous.' Fartnite was the most popular video game in Beanotown history. Kids would do almost anything to set a new high score.

Angel Face nodded, 'Sure was. But you

qualify for mate's rates.' Angel Face winked
dramatically as she said the last two words.

Minnie, Dan and Dennis instantly handed
Angel Face her standard fee. A prized Fumey
the Flaming Fumicorn Exploding Butt sweet –
from each of them.

When groan–ups claim sweets can be bad for your health, they're talking about these beauties . . . just a bit SPICY! – The Ed

She produced a brown cardboard folder from her school bag. It was a private investigator's case file.

'In here is the result of me snooping on Whelan.'

Minnie's eyes widened when she saw what was written neatly on the cover.

Dennis spotted it too. 'Huh! So much for you solving the mystery of Whelan. I want my sweet back. You can't even spell mystery.'

Angel Face sighed. 'No refunds.' She quickly licked each of the sweets as insurance. She looked at Minnie and Dan. 'Do you guys want to tell him, or shall I?'

The report flipped open as Dan slid it across. Dennis couldn't stop himself from yelling out. 'Whelan's not the teacher's pet! He's the teacher's kid!'

DUN! DUN! DUN!

The whole canteen hushed as they turned to look. Then the buzz restarted, louder than ever with the sound of gossiping.

Chapter Six

THE MYSTERY MAN

Minnie didn't think Miss Mistry seemed old
enough to have a son the age Whelan was.
On a good day, her teacher seemed like a
cool big sister, something Minnie had always
wished for.

After lunch, she spotted Whelan skulking
at the edge of the playground. Thanks to them,
the entire school knew his secret.

'Whassup, Whelan Mistry?' asked Minnie.

'It's Mistry-Mahon,' he replied sulkily.

'You're not a mystery man anymore,
Whelan,' replied Minnie.

'That's my name. Mistry from Mum, and M-A-H-O-N is my dad's surname. It's Irish.'

He explained his parents separated years ago. His mum wanted to spend more time with her elderly grandparents in Beanotown, but his dad didn't want to leave his job in Ireland.

When Miss Mistry was offered her dream job as a teacher at her childhood school and

Whelan's dad refused to move with her, they split up.

Whelan chose to stay with his school mates, teammates and dad in Ireland.

'That must have been tough on Miss . . . your mum,' blurted Minnie.

'Yeah. I think she hoped we might all get back together some day.'

Ever since, Whelan had stayed with his mum in the school holidays. But this was the first time he'd been over during term time. His dad was a professional Super Epic Turbo Cricket player, who'd been picked for the All-Ireland team for the World Cup in Greenland, so Whelan was staying with his mum for a while.

'You guys get away with anything here,' he giggled, shaking his head in wonder.

'Almost anything. Your mum knows most dodges. I think she likes it when we're mischievous, but she stops the destructive stuff. She's cool.'

'Cool?!' Whelan seemed shocked. 'I mean, I love my mum but cool isn't how I'd describe her. Do you think your mum's cool?'

Minnie laughed. 'Nope. Mum gets mad at me even when I do something helpful.'

WHAT DO YOU REALLY THINK OF MY BURGLAR CATCHER, MUM?

'Mine thinks she's smarter than me,' said Whelan. 'I told her it's weird how in schools pupils do all the work, but only teachers get paid and she just smiled and patted me on the head!'

'My mum gets out my baby photos every time I have mates over,' remembered Minnie.

'Snap!' laughed Whelan. 'Why do they do that? It's so embarrassing.'

'My mum's bossy! But she can change her mind as soon as I've done what she's told me to do.' She imitated her mum's voice, a deeper, sterner version of her own. "'Eat your dinner. I want to see a clean plate!'" BUT "Don't LICK it!!!!!'"

Whelan knew exactly what Minnie was talking about. He joined in.

"'Sit still!' THEN "Get a move on!'"

Minnie laughed at Whelan's attempt to impersonate his mum. He'd made his voice go high. It was hilarious. Their mums had loads in common.

'I've had an idea for a new game. Mums' Annoying Sayings. We agree the list and score them off as soon as we hear them,' suggested Minnie.

Whelan agreed. 'You're on. The loser displays their baby photo poster-sized on the school gates.'

And just like that, Minnie and Whelan had become mates, thanks to their mums being . . . mums. She started to draw up the checklist.

'Next time, we'll compare dads . . .'

TOP 10 THINGS MUMS SAY!

1. Sorry isn't good enough!
2. Go to sleep, THIS MINUTE!
3. You are what you eat!
4. I'll treat you like a grown-up when you start acting like one!!
5. That's what happens when you don't listen!
6. You've got no one to blame but YOURSELF!
7. You're not old enough!
8. Look at me when I'm talking to you!
9. If the wind changes, you'll get stuck with that facial expression!
10. BECAUSE I SAY SO!

Chapter Seven

THE CODFATHER

Not for the first time, Minnie couldn't concentrate in class.

After making fun of her mum, she secretly felt a tiny bit guilty. She hardly knew Whelan. Had she over-shared? Nope. She trusted him.

He'd spilled just as much about *his* mum, and she was *her* teacher. They had a parent pact. It felt good to know other kid's grown-ups – even the 'cool' ones – were as baffling as her own.

Minnie couldn't wait to tell her folks she'd been made captain. She was bursting with pride. None of her brothers had achieved this honour. The last Makepeace to make captain was her dad! She was continuing the family legacy. When the bell rang for home time, she bolted.

'Smell you later, Dennis,' she giggled, as her cousin lagged, hobbling after her like Long John Silver.

She rushed into the playground, scanning for her parents.

Every Monday, they collected her straight from school and drove to the Beanotown Mega Chippy for a Codfather Family Fish Feast. She was vegetarian, but this was an offer Minnie never refused.

She thought she heard Mum yelling,
'Minnie, over here!'

But it was Aunty Sandra, 'You're with us
tonight, Min. I've got your stuff.'

Minnie hesitated. She'd normally be thrilled to go to Aunty Sandra's house, but she wanted to tell Mum and Dad her good news.

'I nearly forgot. We're going to Beanotown Mega Chippy on the way back!' added Aunty Sandra. Things were looking up.

But dinner made her feel worse. It was the same Monday meal, but a totally different experience. The Menaces splashed spicy curry sauce over *everything*. Fish, chips, even the banana fritters Minnie had especially picked for dessert.

Dennis Senior kept cracking dad jokes, which Dennis and Aunty Sandra found hilarious. And they were pretty funny, to be fair. But all the laughter made Minnie feel sad.

DENNIS SENIOR'S CHIPPY JOKES

DID YOU HEAR ABOUT THE FIGHT OUTSIDE THE CHIP SHOP? TWO FISH GOT BATTERED.

A WOMAN WALKED INTO A CHIPPY RUN BY TWO PRIESTS. SHE ASKED ONE, 'ARE YOU THE FISH FRIAR?' HE REPLIED, 'NO, I'M THE CHIP MONK!'

WHERE DO THE HEALTHIEST FISH AND CHIPS COME FROM? THE VITAMIN SEA.

WHAT DO YOU CALL A MALE SHEEP THAT WORKS IN A FISH AND CHIPS SHOP? A BATTERING RAM.

'DOCTOR, DOCTOR I THINK I NEED GLASSES!' 'YOU CERTAINLY DO, SIR. THIS IS A FISH AND CHIP SHOP!'

Her mood worsened when she received her 'overnight' bag. It was massive. It was stuffed with enough outfits for a week away. Minnie did the maths; she was staying until after the semi-final. It would be the longest she'd ever been apart from her parents. Something seriously weird was happening.

And what about the semi-finals? Would they even be there? Dennis's dad had made a banner and his kid wasn't even able to play!

After dinner, Minnie phoned home.

Her mum answered. Minnie asked her to grab Dad. She had some exciting news to tell them both.

'Your dad's not able to speak right now.'

'**What?**' asked Minnie. Her mum could easily tell how upset she was by her tone.

Her mum began to sniffle.

'Mum? Are you OK?'

'We've both got a cold, so we're just making sure you stay 100% fit for the semi-final. Especially with Dennis injured.'

'You'll be there Friday?' Minnie thought about telling her mum she was captain, but it didn't feel right without her dad on the call. She'd leave it as a surprise for when they saw her leading the team out, wearing her captain's armband.

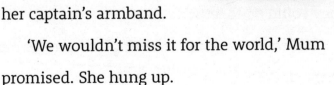

'We wouldn't miss it for the world,' Mum promised. She hung up.

It was raining, so the treehouse was off limits. Minnie was on an inflatable camp bed in Dennis's room. She tossed and turned. But she couldn't doze. Things weren't helped by Dennis regularly parping.

Her Dad had once asked her, 'What could possibly be more annoying than your mum's snoring?' Minnie had finally found the answer: things that go PUMP in the night! She giggled out loud.

It turned out Dennis was still awake too.

Minnie decided to tell him how things had become even worse between her mum and dad.

'Last year, Mum signed them up for a class they could do together.'

'Ballroom dancing or baking?' asked Dennis in the dark.

'Neither. Kung Fu.' Minnie rolled her eyes at the memory.

'They never make each other laugh. They just argue about snoring and pants.'

A low, rumbling, trump echoed across the hallway. It went on, and on, and on. The house shook. When it ended, her uncle loudly said, **'Ta-dah!'**

A few seconds later, a similarly long, high-pitched squeak came from the other room.

Dennis sighed happily. 'My parents are gross. I know what will cheer you up.' He started to chant, as loudly as possible.

'We can hear you farting!'

'We can hear you farting!'

'We can hear you farting!'

Minnie laughed so hard, she cried. His mum and dad were obviously trying to ignore him, pretending they'd done no such thing. Dennis changed his chant.

FARTASTIC!

'We can SMELL you farting . . . '

This time, his parents instantly interrupted. Minnie winced.

'Good! Then I don't have to punish you for still being awake!' shouted Uncle Dennis.

'Go back to sleep, kids!' yelled Aunty Sandra in a pitch as high and squeaky as her fart was.

Dennis turned to Minnie. 'Grown-ups are weird. They clearly find farting as hilarious as kids, but will never admit it. I've never known a kid who doesn't find fart jokes funny.'

Minnie wiped her eyes and blew her nose. Dennis was right. 'If grown-ups laughed openly at farts, the world would be a funnier place,' she said.

She remembered the picture of the Menace

family motto in kitchen downstairs. She'd
stared at it during dinner to take her mind off
the bogging curried fish feast.

Laugh was written largest, the most important part.

The prank she was planning would bring the laughs back. The rest would follow.

She hoped.

Chapter Eight

EPIC FAYLE TIME

Semi-final day arrived quicker than Billy Whizz racing a bullet train.

Minnie was first to the changing rooms. Hanging on a coat hook was a bright neon-yellow armband, stencilled with a large black C, for CAPTAIN.

Minnie carefully stretched it over her bicep. It felt good. She flexed her arm like a bodybuilder and grinned at her reflection in the grubby changing-room mirror.

'This is the biggest day of my whole life.

Write about THIS, Craig and Mike . . . ' she said to herself.

She felt her mouth stretch into a grin as a feeling of giddy happiness took over. Things were going to be alright. The rest of the team started to roll in.

'Looking good, Skipper,' said Jem

'That armband fits you perfectly,' added Mandi appreciatively.

'That's because it's elastic.' Typical Rubi. She never let good vibes get in the way of the scientific truth. But they all knew Minnie deserved this.

'Settle down, team.' It was Miss Mistry. Whelan was traipsing behind, carrying a large flipchart, which he set up in the far corner. Meanwhile, his mum gathered the team around her. 'It's time to talk tactics.'

She nodded to Whelan, who flipped open the first page on the flip chart.

Miss Mistry was a former Bash Street pupil and had studied the Art of Mischief at college. She knew what happened off the pitch was as important as what occurred on it. Especially when you were up against your oldest, bitterest rivals: Beanotown Academy.

The last time the teams had met, Bash Street had clinched a narrow victory, so it was likely the Academy wanted revenge.

The rivalry between the schools had grown toxic following a disastrous experiment from Mayor Brown when Beanotown Academy threatened to takeover Bash Street School.

BARBARA BUTTSQUEAK

TIM DIMM

PEREGRINE POT-ROAST

JOYCE FOYCE

SPOTTY SPUDKIN

BARRY BULLWHIP

'Whelan's our secret weapon,' continued

Miss Mistry. 'They've never seen him play for

us before.' She turned towards her son. 'Don't touch the ball in the first half. Let them think we can't cope without Dennis.'

Minnie kept quiet. Whelan not stealing her limelight for the first half worked for her!

'But why would we do that?' asked Whelan doubtfully.

'Because I say so!' his mum replied.

Whelan smiled broadly at Minnie. He winked and gave her a cheeky thumbs up.

She couldn't believe it; he'd just won their little competition. That was the last weird mum phrase he'd needed to complete the set. Whatever happened today, the entire school would be laughing at her embarrassing baby poster next week!

Miss Mistry explained, 'Because we want

to lull them into a false sense of security and then attack. Barry Bullwhip won't know what's hit the back of his net!'

As Minnie led the team out, she looked for her parents, but she couldn't spot them.

The ref was the Academy's fearsome cyborg teacher, Mr Fayle, who had recently lost what had become known as The Battle for Bash Street School (available in all good bookshops – and some rubbish ones too).

He'd lived up to his name and slunk back to the Academy. The Bash Street supporters were holding handmade banners that made fun of the nickname they'd awarded him.

MR FAYLE: FIRST NAME – EPIC.

Fayle snarled. He silently vowed revenge against Bash Street School. He'd coached his team to play dirty and as he was the ref, there was nothing that could be done to stop them. The trick started as soon as Beanotown Academy mounted their first attack.

Joyce Foyce squirted chilli sauce into Rubi's face, who then dropped the ball in front of the onrushing Tim Dimm.

1-0 TO BEANOTOWN ACADEMY.

Fayle also 'never spotted' pesky Peregrine Pot-Roast pouring itching powder down Jem's back. She looked as if she was dancing in a weird celebration, instead of marking Joyce Foyce, who scored another tap-in.

2-0 TO BEANOTOWN ACADEMY.

Minnie was furious. She hadn't touched the ball. The game was racing away. Was she about to go down in history as the worst captain ever?

'Jem, stop dancing and start defending! Don't cry Rubi, we can still do it.'

Minnie hadn't noticed the underhand tricks, and she was about to become the next victim. The tactic of holding Whelan in reserve was stupid. They needed him now.

Minnie chased every ball, determined to keep them from scoring again, to give her team a fighting chance in the second half.

It worked until Fayle cunningly extended a robotic leg, making Minnie tumble in front of a wayward shot from Tim Dimm. She careered forward, taking the ball to the face, which bounced off and straight past Rubi into the back of her own goal.

3-0 TO BEANOTOWN ACADEMY.

What a butt-clenching embarrassment. There was no coming back from this!

The Academy's supporters were triumphant, as Fayle blew for half-time.

As Minnie trudged off, she still couldn't spot her parents.

Miss Mistry was furious at the dirty tricks.

'Poor Rubi's eyes are still streaming. There's no way she can continue,' she fumed.

Minnie, finally aware of the sneaky pranks, felt a meltdown building.

Miss Mistry challenged her to turn her anger into positive energy for the second half. 'Whelan, it's time to sting back.'

What followed was legendary!

Five minutes to the end of the game and they were level. A hat-trick from Minnie, after three Whelan assists! It was like they telepathically understood what each other was about to do before they did it. They were so good, there was nothing the Beanotown Academy players, or Fayle, could do to stop them!

'What a performance by the player on loan from Legwee Dribblers. From first-half zero to second-half hero!' commentated Stevie Star, who was running another livestream after the success of his last video – #welovewhelan was still trending!

Back in Legwee, the whole of Whelan's 'other' school was watching, willing him on. It worked. Whelan put Bash Street into a 4-3 lead with his scorpion kick! 'BA-BA-BOOM! Scor-pi-oh!' yelled Stevie.

But the celebrations stopped when Fayle disallowed the goal, with no explanation.

'NO GOAL!' shrieked Harsha. Fans watching suspected another prank, but it was true.

Minnie couldn't believe it. There was nothing wrong with the goal – it was a beaut! Whelan was holding his head in his hands. The Academy players and fans were wildly cheering in triumph.

There was a commotion on the side-lines. Mrs Clamp, the mean head teacher at the Academy was squabbling with someone. Very loudly and extremely rudely. 'Scorpion kicks are illegal, you **FOOL**. They're unsavable!'

'That's the whole point! How very dare you talk about unfairness!' replied an irate Mrs Creecher.

The whole crowd, all the players and everyone watching online were now focussed upon the touchline. Head teachers arguing! **Wow!** The ultimate end-level boss battle.

'Let's settle this the old way,' said Mrs Creecher, stretching her arms.

She adored ancient rules, as any Bash Street School pupil could confirm. She was clenching an antique copy of the Super Epic Turbo Cricket Manual.

'In ancient battles, a champion from each side could be nominated to fight each other, instead of their armies. It saved a lot of extra cleaning up. In the event of a draw, the same happens in this sport, so I nominate . . . **ME!**'

'I choose Mr Fayle!' Mrs Clamp tossed her head, smirking at her genius.

Creecher shook her head. 'No, the champion must be of equal rank. Unless Mr Fayle has been promoted, and you *demoted* . . . it's me versus you. "Head" to "head".'

Mrs Clamp looked disgusted. 'But I've never fought anyone before. The last thing I'd wish for is any unpleasantness.'

'Any more last wishes?' asked Creecher, as she rolled her sleeves up. 'It's not a fight. The combat in Super Epic Turbo Cricket is the noble art of the DANCE OFF.'

Stevie didn't need to be asked to unleash some happening beats. This was going viral. He pressed record.

'A dance off? No way.' Mrs Clamp sat down and crossed her arms.

'Get up this instant! I'm going to teach you a lesson you'll never forget!' Mrs Creecher screeched at Mrs Clamp.

She started throwing shapes. It reminded Minnie of when she used to teach them maths.

The crowd started chanting in time with her movements.

BIG FISH
LITTLE FISH
CARDBOARD BOX

The fans went wild. What a dancer!
She moved forward doing the Griddy, then
moonwalked back across to Mrs Clamp.

'Follow that!' Mrs Creecher ordered.

Mrs Clamp started to ballroom dance with Mr Fayle. Their moves were unintentionally hilarious. Mr Fayle became so embarrassed, he short-circuited.

The last words he uttered before conking out and falling to the floor were: 'Match awarded to Bash Street School.'

Minnie was elated. The team she'd captained was through to the final.

BUT still neither of Minnie's parents were anywhere to be seen. They'd lied to her. Already, her mind was tweaking her prank recipe to add just a dash of revenge.

Tonight, she'd be sleeping with the Menaces again.

Tomorrow, she'd unleash maximum mischief on her parents!

Chapter Nine

THE GREATEST PRANK IN BEANOTOWN HISTORY

Minnie woke before dawn. It was Saturday. No school. She felt excited and there were butterflies in her stomach, just like on Christmas mornings.

She stretched and realised her body ached. Most days she'd have dived back underneath the covers, but this was the day she was going to unleash the biggest, funniest and messiest prank of her life.

She unfolded a large diagram of her house, waking Dennis in the process.

It was covered with notes, lines and symbols. They were all scribbled in Minnie's scruffy handwriting.

Dennis didn't complain, stretching and yawning as he said, 'I love the smell of pranks in the morning.'

The Menace household started to stir. A mahoosive rasping pump from Dennis Senior woke up Bea, who unleashed a yodelling wail that Gnasher responded to with a howl. Total chaos, which meant no chance of them checking in upon Minnie or Dennis. It was still dark as they snuck outside.

They'd stashed their supplies in the garden shed the night before.

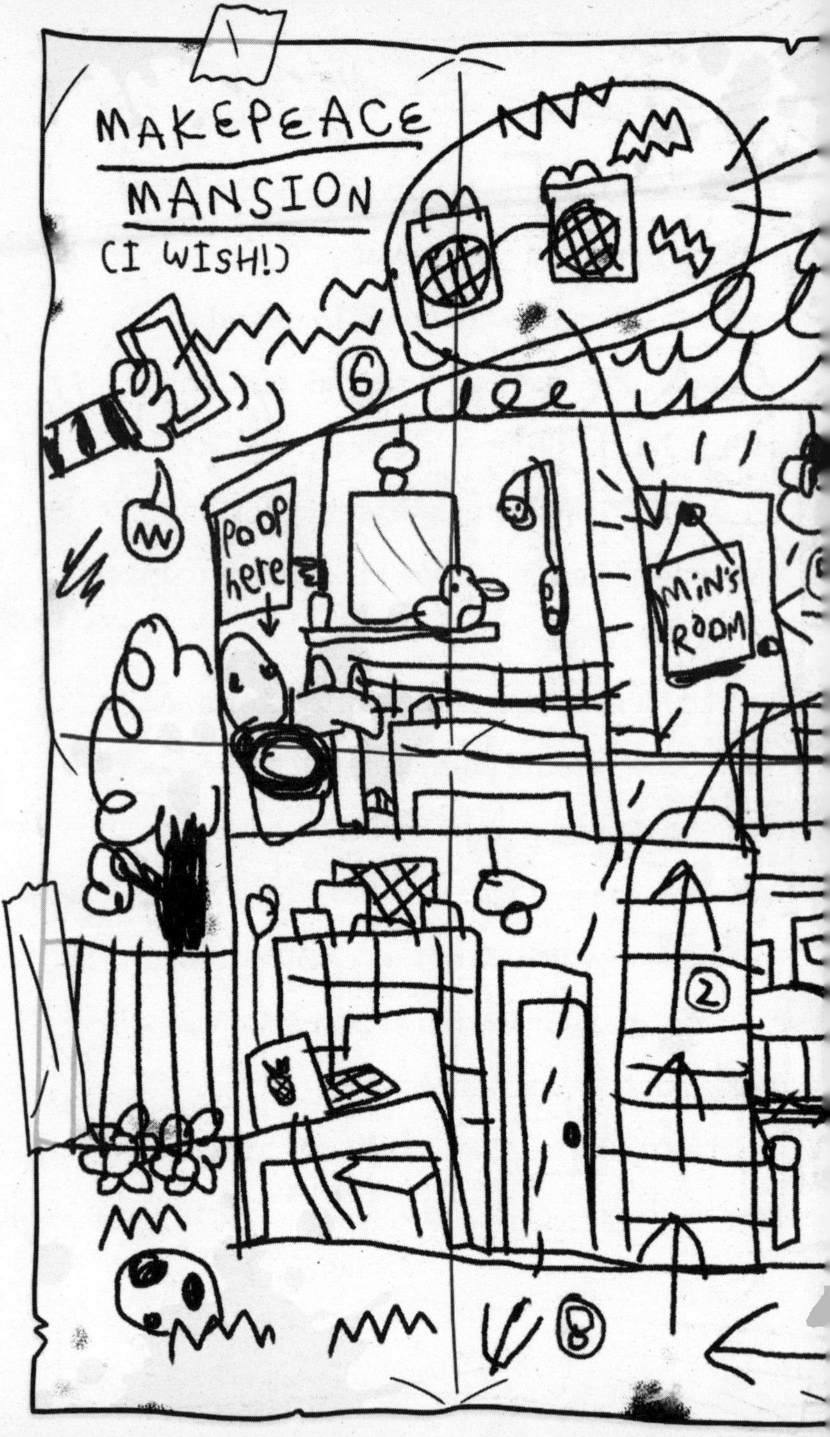
MAKEPEACE MANSION
(I WISH!)
6
poop here
Min's ROOM
2
8

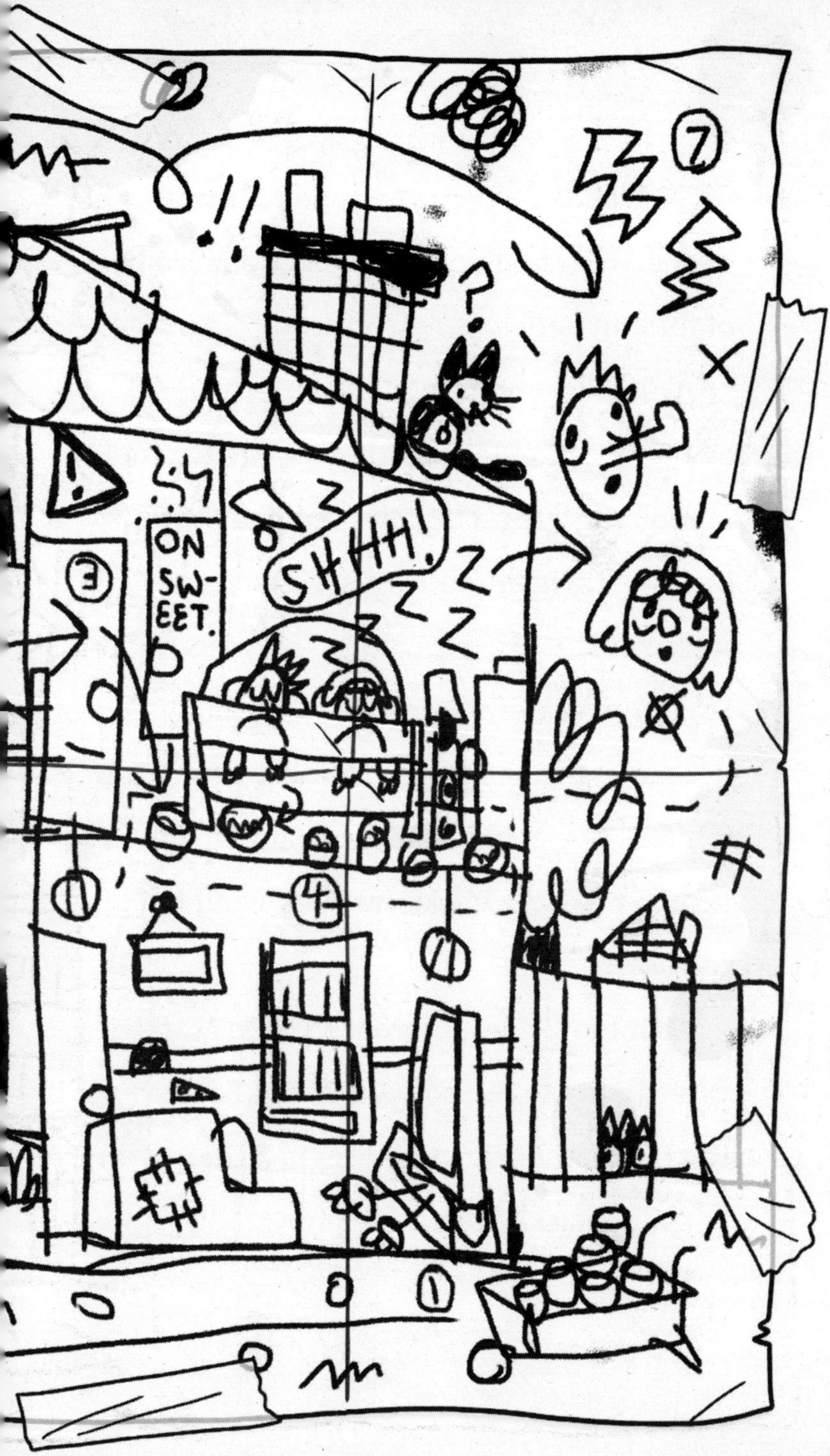

ON SW-EET.
SHHH!

'Careful,' Dennis warned Minnie as he opened the shed door. 'My dad hoards a heap of junk in here.'

One false move would result in an avalanche of empty paint pots, broken tools and old toys tumbling down upon them, burying their mischievous mission in seconds.

Dennis carefully unlocked the bulging door and grinned widely. Minnie gave a low whistle. She could hear the beat of her own heart. 'RESULT! I knew Mark wouldn't let me down.'

Minnie's eldest brother Mark is Marketing Director at the Beanotown Baked Beans Factory. Famously, he'd designed their award-winning packaging.

He'd recently signed a deal with the mayor to remove the first 'O' from the Beanotown sign on Mount Beano.

Smart as he was though, he'd never
checked the small print in his contract. He was
paid entirely in beans. Five hundred tins per
week! He loved eating them, but he always had
leftovers about to go out of date.

When Minnie mentioned that she needed a
hundred tins for a school project, he'd come up

trumps – trumping was a very regular thing for Mark Makepeace, given his diet.

Minnie started passing the tins, one by one, to Dennis who piled them into a wheelbarrow. Minnie grabbed a stack of paper cups. They snuck across the road with Gnasher and hid in Minnie's front garden.

The idea was to surround her parents' bed – in fact their entire bedroom floor – with paper cups full of baked beans. The idea was to make them get up quickly in the dark and watch them zoom straight into a baked-bean slip and slide!

'Oh, butt squeaks, I forgot the tin opener,' mumbled Dennis.

Minnie couldn't believe it.

'You. Had. One. Job.'

Gnasher dashed between them. He grabbed a tin between his paws and chomped the top off with his super-tough teeth. **Result!**

Dennis started to fill the cups and Minnie zipped in and out, silently sneaking up and down the stairs, between her bean supply and her parents' bedroom.

She heard the drone of her mum snoring. **Result!** This was going to be easier than she imagined. Minnie took care to place the paper cups of beans all around her parents' bedroom.

'Uh Oh.' Minnie suddenly spotted a problem. Dad wasn't in bed! Was he in the small bathroom at the other side of the room? She backed out slowly, edging towards the door. 'Phew!' She was sweating.

Lastly, Minnie had to switch on the portable speaker in her room. This was the key to triggering the prank. She'd created a sound file that would guarantee her dozy parents rushed straight into her trap.

Minnie crept across the hallway and opened the door to her own bedroom.

She froze. Dad was sleeping in her bed, his feet sticking out awkwardly. At first it looked comical.

Minnie looked closer. He was sucking his thumb again. In fact, it looked like he was about to chew straight through it. A grim frown ruled his face.

Well, she was about to turn that frown upside-down. Thankfully, she had plenty of beans to spare!

Once she was done boobytrapping her room too, she stood for a moment and

wondered why her dad was in here. Was it

mum's snoring again?

Then he pumped. It was time for another

sharp exit. She grabbed her speaker, then

placed it on the landing between the rooms

and turned it up to full volume, ready to be

activated. Everything was ready.

When Minnie returned outside, Gnasher

was lying dazed in the wheelbarrow, covered in bean juice. Dennis explained her brother had mistakenly included twenty tins of beans with mini sausages.

Gnasher had gone into a feeding frenzy when he'd opened them all, resulting in a full belly and a lot of trapped wind. They'd have to wheel him back to the treehouse to let him recover where Dennis's parents wouldn't find – or smell – him.

But first, Minnie produced a massive balloon and a funnel. Dennis helped pour the remaining tins of beans and the juice from the empties into it. They attached it above the front door. It bulged and wobbled. She loved her parents equally, so this would guarantee they both got the full super-epic **Bean-OH prank** treatment!

'Let's get this party started,' said Minnie. She knew her parent's alarm clock was set for 7:00. The time was 6:58. It was now or never. Minnie pressed play on SpotOnFly, her phone's music app. She found the file called: Mum and Dad's Worst Lesson Ever!

'Your phone's hooked up to the speaker?' checked Dennis. Minnie nodded and pressed play. A terrifying voice boomed out of the

speaker on the landing, so loudly that
it echoed around the entire house
and garden.

**GET UP THIS INSTANT! I'M GOING TO TEACH
YOU A LESSON YOU'LL NEVER FORGET!**

**GET UP THIS INSTANT! I'M GOING TO TEACH
YOU A LESSON YOU'LL NEVER FORGET!**

GET UP THIS INSTANT! I'M GOING TO TEACH
YOU A LESSON YOU'LL NEVER FORGET!

Both her parents had been taught by
Mrs Creecher, back when she was a terror.
They'd told Minnie they still had nightmares
about her yelling at them.

Minnie persuaded Stevie to give her the
sound file from the semi-final dance off!
It was mischievous genius from Minnie.
It guaranteed them jumping to attention
immediately, without a second thought.

Minnie sniggered as she heard her mum slipping on the beans, cursing as she struggled to suss out what was happening. It was the ultimate rude awakening. Dennis and Minnie rolled around on the grass, laughing loudly.

Mum emerged from the house already covered, followed by Dad straight behind her. So far, he'd dodged the worst of the beans . . .

'I'll soon fix that,' smirked Minnie, as she loaded her trusty peashooter. She aimed at the balloon she'd prepared, filled to bursting point, just above Dad's head.

Veeesht . . . POP! 'Gotcha!'

Beans flew everywhere. Dennis produced an umbrella to avoid the worst of the blast.

'It's raining beans, hallelujah!' laughed Minnie gleefully.

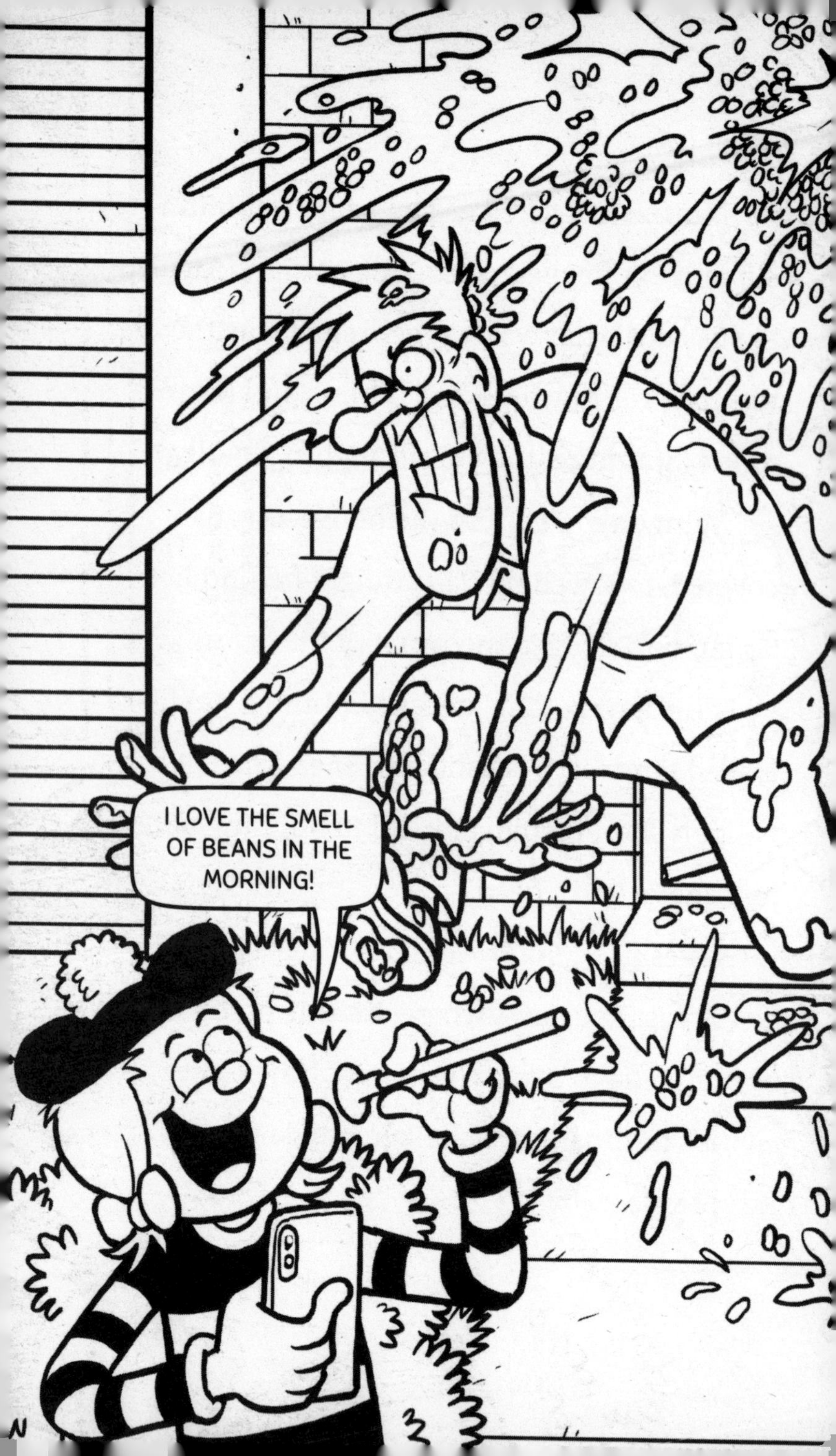
I LOVE THE SMELL OF BEANS IN THE MORNING!

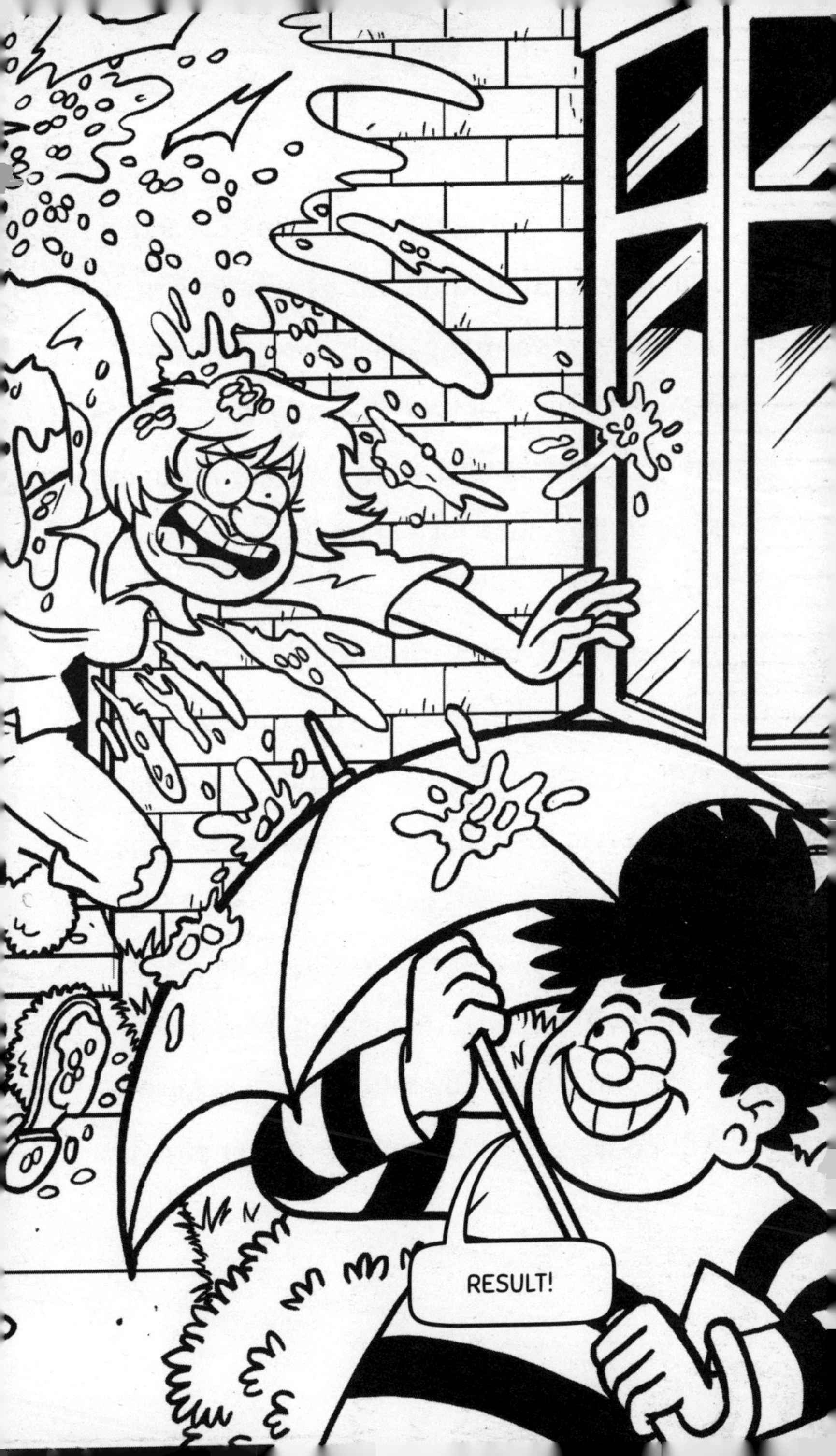
RESULT!

A torrent of bright orange gunk drenched Dad, showering Mum with a fresh dose in the process. Minnie paused the speaker and snapped a pic. Her brother would love this! So would Harsha! She couldn't wait to claim her place in Har Har's Joke Shop Pranking Hall of Fame later!

Best of all, her Mum and Dad would be laughing together. For the first time in ages!

Except they weren't. Laughter was what Minnie had visualised – the reality was the complete opposite. They were raging! They marched straight over. Bean juice dripping from their hair, steam gushing from their ears.

'Er, how have you **bean**?' asked Minnie. Still no laughs. She'd never seen her parents so angry!

'I think you're both great human **beans**,' said Dennis.

'You're toast. You too, Dennis. You wait until your parents hear about this!' replied his favourite aunty. She wasn't trying to make a joke though and became even angrier when he smirked. She grabbed the sleeve of his jumper and yanked him sharply up.

'**Ouch**,' he complained.

Then something happened. Minnie started to sob. Everyone stopped in their tracks.

Dennis turned to his aunty and uncle and angrily shouted, 'Minnie's upset because you two

never laugh anymore!' His voice shook.

Minnie's parent's faces fell and their anger drained away.

'Dennis, could you pop back across the road and tell your mum you're my favourite nephew?' Minnie's mum said softly.

'Eh? I'm your only nephew?'

'GO,' she snapped.

Dennis pushed the wheelbarrow with Gnasher in it back home, thinking how weird grown-ups are.

Minnie's parents swept her up into a big group hug.

'Let's go inside. We need to talk,' her dad said gently.

At the table, Minnie's parents confirmed her deepest fear: they were getting a divorce.

Though the signs were all there, she never thought it would happen to her parents. Minnie heard everything they said but she didn't fully listen. Her brain was whirring, trying to figure out why it had happened.

'Is it my fault? Did I prank you too much?' Minnie asked.

'Of course not! You've done nothing wrong,' Mum said.

'Well, a few things wrong,' Dad said, picking a rogue bean out of his ear. 'But nothing that caused this,' he was quick to add.

'And you're sure this prank hasn't **bean** enough to change your mind?' she asked with a hopeful smile.

Minnie's parents laughed, but sadly shook their heads.

'So what now?' she asked.

'Mum's moving in with Miss Mistry until she finds a new place. You're staying here with me if that's OK?' explained Dad.

'Miss Mistry?!' Minnie was stunned. Miss Mistry had grown up next door to her dad, and Mum and her did coffee and cake occasionally, but Minnie always thought it was by way of apology for her mischief. She didn't know they were actually . . . friends! She shuddered at the thought.

It was too much to take in.

That evening Mum ordered a takeaway to cheer everyone up. It didn't work. Minnie played with her food.

It was the Makepeace Family's last supper.

Minnie's heart was breaking. Nothing was ever going to be the same again.

Chapter Ten

WHELAN'S DOUBLE TROUBLE

Minnie's mind raced in class, her thoughts crashing into one another.

At break, Whelan rushed towards her. He was sporting his usual grin, with an extra-mischievous twinkle sprinkled on top!

'How did it go?'

Minnie's glum expression said it all. 'It couldn't have gone worse if Calamity James had arranged things.'

She blurted out everything. She watched Whelan's jaw drop with each new detail. Well, all except for her mum moving in with him.

'It's going to be weird not having both of my parents telling me off in unison.'

Whelan took a deep breath.

'It's maybe not as terrible as you think?'

Minnie looked at him as if a massive boil was swelling on his nose, ready to burst. But she listened as he explained how gutted he'd been when his own parents had split.

'It's tough at first. When Mum left, Dad said it was because she didn't love us anymore.'

'That's a fib,' said Minnie. She could clearly see how much Miss Mistry loved her son.

'I didn't know what to believe. Mum said they'd loved each other when they had me, but marriages are like tadpoles; you've got to let

them go if they turn into frogs.'

'What?!' Minnie laughed. 'That makes no sense: all tadpoles turn into frogs.'

'That's what I said! But I guess what matters is that she still loves me just the same, even if she doesn't love my dad anymore,' Whelan said. 'Besides, living with my dad is a lot of fun, and my mum always puts loads of effort in to making sure the holidays are packed with fun things. '

'I'm staying with my dad too,' said Minnie.

'What about your mum?'

'Erm, I've got a surprise for you.'

Whelan raised an eyebrow. He hated surprises.

'You remember how we compared our mums' most annoying habits?'

He nodded.

'My mum's moving in at your place,' Minnie grinned. 'Do you think you can handle it?'

'No way! I can always head back to Ireland,' Whelan laughed. 'Wait a second. What's your mum called?'

'Vicky, why?'

Whelan smacked his forehead. 'My mum said "Vic" was moving in. I thought she had a new boyfriend! What a relief!'

Minnie laughed, and some of the weight she'd been carrying lifted. Whelan had been so easy to talk to. He knew how she was feeling.

'If you want to keep it a secret, I promise I won't tell anyone. If someone spots your mum at our house, I'll say she's just asking Mum for extra homework for you.'

Minnie chewed it over. There was no way anyone would believe *that*.

'Honesty's best,' decided Minnie. 'Unless I've done something *really* bad!'

She told the rest of the team before training. None of them knew quite what to say as they'd not been through it before, but that didn't matter when they all came in for a big group hug. Minnie knew they were there for her.

As they broke from the huddle, Whelan spotted his mum approaching. She looked worried. He smiled and nodded towards Minnie to let her know he knew what was going on and was fine with it. She shot him a relieved wink of appreciation.

She clapped her hands sharply to get her team's attention. 'We've just discovered our opponents for the final. It's going to be the toughest test imaginable.'

'Worse than maths?' asked Minnie doubtfully – she sucked at maths.

'Much, much worse.' It was Stevie with the update. He'd watched the livestream with Harsha. 'Bogwarts School of Magical Mayhem, from Transylvania, just beat Fake Madrid 23-0.'

'Bogwarts?' chuckled Minnie. 'Sounds like something you'd catch from a dirty loo seat.'

'They petrify opponents,' warned Harsha. 'Their tactic is to scare first, score later.'

'We're going to have to invent our own magical mischief to stand a chance then,' Minnie pointed out.

Chapter Eleven

THE CURE FOR BOGWARTS!

The build-up to the final was manic. The most exciting fortnight of Minnie's life.

Home life was way better than expected. Dad coached her every night. He was living his own childhood dreams through his daughter. Minnie realised Dad was a better cook, but her mum had obviously been the expert in doing the washing without shrinking everything.

She had dinner with Mum twice a week. It was great fun hanging out with Whelan too.

Mum took her shopping at the weekend.

She got new trainers, a red-and-black stripy tracksuit, and had even been allowed to get her ears pierced. If she wanted. Which she didn't. Minnie remembered the time Dennis had done one of his with a school stapler. OUCH! No thanks!

Do NOT try this at home! – The Ed

She was spending more fun time with her parents than ever before. It was brilliant! Even her brothers had started to check in on her. She'd never been made such a fuss over. Mum and Dad both seemed happier too. Sure, things weren't quite as good as when they'd all lived happily together, but Minnie was starting to realise that they weren't half as bad as she'd feared either.

But the main subject on everyone in

Beanotown's minds was the final. All the shops were decorated in Bash Street School colours and Minnie had received hundreds of good luck messages.

Stevie Star had edited together a video of their opponents. Harsha shared it with the team. It looked like a horror movie. They had a vampire, a werewolf and a zombie as star players! 'They dial up regular pranks beyond funny, into nasty,' she told them.

Minnie and her teammates suffered nightmares after watching Stevie's edits of Bogwarts' previous matches.

She teased Jem. 'Don't become Hellenor Killmore's pre-match protein shake.'

'It seems Wolfgang Feist puts extra bite into his tackles,' Jem replied with a smirk.

'You'd better watch out, Rubes,' added Whelan. 'I've heard Chewie Suarez prefers brains!'

Rubi nodded nervously.

Whelan started to stagger, his arms stretched out in front of him, as he twisted his mouth and made yucky moaning, slurpy sounds in his best impression of a zombie.

Miss Mistry interrupted. 'Harsha's taking us through some special training before the final.'

'But Harsha's never played a match. How can she coach us?' protested Dennis. He'd been hoping Miss Mistry was going to ask him to coach. He was feeling left out due to his injury.

'We're going to out *prank* them,' replied Harsha confidently. 'Give them the giggles. They're not used to laughing. They take themselves too seriously.' She looked at Dennis. 'Do you still have the ball Gnasher burst in Ireland? I'd like to borrow it, please.'

Minnie was getting apprehensive. A burst ball and coach who'd never played the game. Was this really going to work?

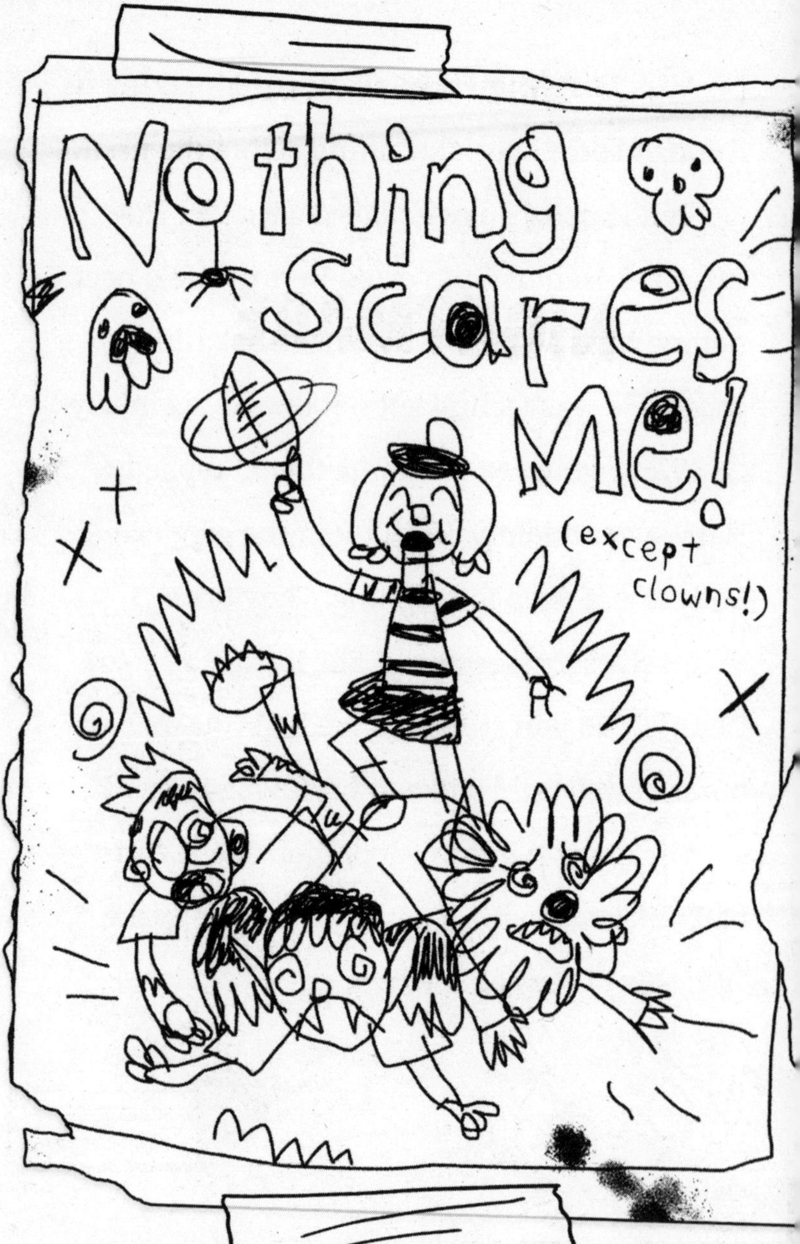
Nothing Scares Me!
(except clowns!)

Chapter Twelve

MINNIE'S FINAL NIGHTMARE

Bash Street school hosted the game again.

On the live stream, the Bogwarts team was introduced by Stevie.

MUMMY – Faye Row

ZOMBIE – hewie Suarez

GORGON – Medusa Gorgon

SCARY CLOWN – Penny Smart

WEREWOLF – Wolfgang Feist

VAMPIRE – Hellenor Killmore

Pre-match, Harsha made them all chew garlic bubblegum from Har Har's Joke Shop, just in case.

As Minnie led the team out, she spotted her parents, faces alive with excitement. Standing behind them were all five of her brothers. They'd stretched out a homemade banner: **MINNIE'S GONNA GET YOU!**

Bogwarts' head teacher Drusilla Kong, was the ref. She was an even scarier sight than Mr Fayle had been. Her hair was woven on top of her head like a ram's horns. But it was her eyes that got Minnie's attention. They glowed orange like dangerous little fires.

She was plastered in thick, chalky white make-up that disguised her deep wrinkles. Or it would have, if she hadn't moved. Instead, it

was a face of a hundred cracks. It only made her look more terrifying.

I TEACH LESSONS NOBODY DARES FORGET!

MINNIE'S GONNA GET YOU!

Minnie whispered to Rubi, 'She's old. Not Creecher-level old. Centuries old!'

Bogwarts' captain was Medusa Gorgon.

From a distance, it looked as if she had curly hair like Whelan, but up close you realised it was a writhing mass of deadly snakes. Real snakes that hissed, rattled and tried to bite anyone who moved too close. The ultimate bad hair day.

'I've got a special conditioner that might help with that,' offered Whelan, who for once didn't follow up with a cheeky wink. That's because anyone who gazed into her eyes was instantly turned to stone!

Harsha had turned something into stone too. She'd filled the deflated ball Gnasher had burst in Legwee with cement. Her classmates helped lift it to the centre spot.

> Again, you REALLY shouldn't do this at home. – The Ed

So, when Chewie Suarez kicked-off, he booted the 'Toe-breaker 2000'.

'PAINSSS,' moaned Chewie, as he collapsed to the ground in agony.

The wailing zombie was helped off the pitch, with a separate stretcher for his detached throbbing toes.

'Watch out! It's the zombie big-toe-collapse,' laughed Dennis.

Harsha's pranking plan was working!

The real ball appeared, and the game restarted, with the opposition one player down. Harsha knew the sub was a vampire and couldn't be used unless . . .

Mysterious, dark clouds gathered.

Disaster! The ref was mumbling a spell! Talk about biased! It was now gloomy enough to bring on Hellenor Killmore. Minnie spotted her rising from a giant kit bag underneath the substitute bench, teeth glinting in the darkness.

But Harsha had planned for *everything*.

With a flick of a switch, she illuminated the pitch with portable sun beds she'd borrowed from Beanotown's tanning salon.

PFOOTFT!

Hellenor transformed into a bat, squeaked angrily, then swifly fluttered back into her dark kit bag. Killmore was no more.

I FEEL LIKE A SUCKER, NOW!

Bash Street took the lead with their first attack of the game, Whelan gripping the ball between his ankles, before backflipping past Faye Rowe and into the goal!

1-0 BASH STREET!

As Whelan rose to celebrate, an angry Faye pushed him into the goalpost.

DONG. The crowd winced at the sound of his knee crashing into metal.

Minnie yelled for her mum to check Whelan over. The first-aid training she'd taken after several of Minnie's more risky pranks was handy in these situations.

Faye came to loom over Vicky as she checked on Whelan's knee. Weirdly, Mum focussed more on the goalkeeper than Whelan's injury.

'Hi. I'm Minnie's, er "mummy". You look very, erm, wound up,' she said.

Faye Rowe just stared back.

So Mum tried cracking a joke. 'My brother's Mindiana Bones, the archaeologist. He discovered an ancient mummy covered in chocolate, nuts and wrapped in gold.'

Faye's face twitched in confusion. She clearly didn't get it. Minnie's mum had her attention though.

'Pharaoh Rocher!' Vicky giggled at her comedy genius. 'Geddit?'

Faye didn't laugh. Harsha's plan was failing. Or was it?

Mum was still talking. 'Is that loo roll stuck to your foot?'

Mum bent down and started to unravel a tiny bit of bandage. Just enough to wrap around a juicy sausage Harsha had secretly supplied. It looked like Faye now had a sausage roll on her toe.

'Looks like your game is up,' Vicky said to Whelan, and she helped him limp off the pitch.

Calamity James subbed on.

The whistle blew, and suddenly Gnasher dashed on, heading straight for the goalkeeper. Dennis shrugged unhelpfully when Drusilla Kong ordered him to get Gnasher 'back' on his lead.

'Since when has Gnasher been on a lead?'

Faye spun like a top as Gnasher nabbed the sausage, before dashing away, causing her bandages to rapidly unwind.

As Gnasher ran off, Wolfgang lurched over, trying to introduce himself via the traditional international doggy welcome greeting: the butt sniff! The fans howled louder than Wolfgang – it was hilarious.

Gnasher was having none of it! He was eating! He disappeared into the crowd, with Wolfgang in hot pursuit, spectators entangled in Faye's yucky ancient bandages.

She'd disappeared completely, either into ancient dust, or to the changing rooms to find some clothing.

Bogwarts were down to two players! Mum had played an important (sausage) role when Minnie needed her most.

The game continued, and Medusa raced towards Rubi, balancing the ball among the snakes on her head between bounces. It was impossible to tackle . . . or even look at her!

She slithered the ball in the goal for a dastardly equaliser! **1-1!**

Medusa **HISSED** in celebration at the Bash Street fans who wisely turned their backs as she goaded them. Apart from one.

Minnie's dad had stuck his palm out, inviting a high five. Medusa slapped it, HARD.

'OUCH! No need for a hissy fit,' complained Darren Makepeace.

Medusa shrugged. 'Why does everyone hate snakes? They're 'armless.'

'Let's show there's no hard feelings with a nice selfie, eh?' asked Dad.

He quickly moved his camera phone, so Medusa's face filled the screen, in gruesome high definition.

'**Wow!** What amazing eyes I—'

She never finished her sentence, because she'd turned herself to stone!

Dad removed the prank specs he'd been wearing – the type kids wore in class to fool teachers into thinking they were awake – and handed them to Harsha.

Minnie's parents were awesome. They'd united to put her best interests at heart.

Chapter Thirteen

FEARS OF A CLOWN

> I'VE GOT A HUNCH SOMETHING UNLUCKY IS ABOUT TO HAPPEN TO ME...

Only Penny Smart, the scary clown, stood between Minnie's team and glory. With her teammates eliminated, Penny had big shoes to fill. Easy for a clown.

Her gigantic feet helped her tackle, block and hack.

It was no laughing matter for Bash Street as Penny played one mean prank after another.

She squirted hot sauce into Mandi's face from the fake flower she was wearing. Poor Mandi joined Whelan pitch side for first aid.

HER WEED WEEWEED ON ME!

Calamity James was already on as the only sub. But his game ended after Penny's spinning bow tie sprayed itching powder over him.

'That disgusting boy has fleas!' she screeched, as James itched uncontrollably.

Drusilla Kong ordered him off for an early bath!

'It's still three versus one, don't worry,' yelled Miss Mistry.

But it wasn't that way for long. Penny faceplanted Jem with a vicious clown-shoe

trip, before
tying a bunch of
helium balloons
to her ankle.

Jem floated high above
the pitch, tantalisingly out
of reach of a swaying
human pyramid
attempting a rescue.

It was a cunning
distraction, so Penny could
attack Rubi with a cunning fib.

COACH SAID TO
FLOAT AROUND THE
MIDFIELD...

'She deliberately squished my poor ickle
foot,' squeaked Penny, pointing at Rubi
accusingly. She'd inhaled helium from a spare
balloon for added cuteness.

Minnie knew it was a lie. Penny was

172

playacting. She'd even painted a massive tear on her cheek and changed the make-up around her mouth to look sad.

But Rubi looked furious and was wearing massive boxing gloves, which didn't help her case.

LEMME AT HER!

'**OFF**!' ordered Drusilla Kong. Rubi's jaw dropped at the sheer injustice.

Penny winked slyly. A shiver ran down Minnie's spine. She called for a time out.

She dashed over to Miss Mistry.

'This is my worst nightmare ever. I'm terrified of clowns,' she whispered.

Miss Mistry understood that fear all too well. A fear fuelled by scary movies, horrid Halloween make-up . . . and terrible jokes. What *wasn't* there to be scared of?

'Minnie, you are the fiercest girl I know. Look how you've handled everything with your parents. You are a warrior. You can do anything. Now take the clown down and win us this cup!'

Minnie realised her teacher was right. She

was Minnie Makepeace, daughter of Darren and Vicky Makepeace. If her parents could get crafty, then so could she!

'OUCH!' Minnie nearly jumped out of her skin as something stung the back of her neck. A vampire bat?!

Nope. Just a paper aeroplane, thrown by Harsha, who was giving her the thumbs up.

Minnie unfolded it and discovered a note from her friend.

Penny Smart has no supernatural powers. She's just a regular kid pretending to be a scary clown. Make her a FUNNY clown, by telling a clown joke.

Minnie wracked her brain. Years ago, Mum and Dad told her clown jokes, so she'd laugh at them instead of being scared. They hadn't worked then, but maybe they would now that she was older? She'd scribbled them down in her diary. In fact they were on the very first page.

She tried to remember some as she bounced the ball towards the Bogwarts' penalty area, where Penny was guarding her goal. There was less than minute left. This would be the final attack. The page flashed before her eyes!

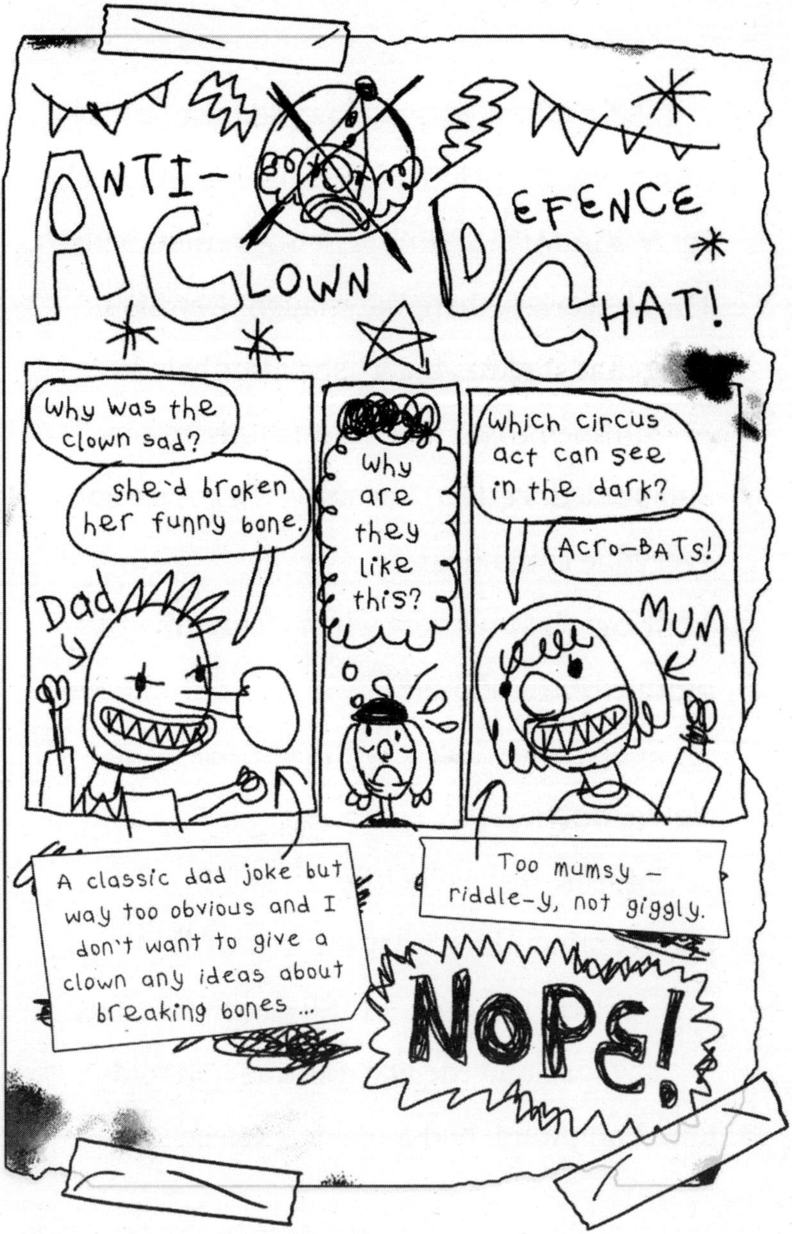
ANTI-CLOWN DEFENCE CHAT!
Why was the clown sad?
She'd broken her funny bone.
Dad
Why are they like this?
Which circus act can see in the dark?
ACRO-BATS!
MUM
A classic dad joke but way too obvious and I don't want to give a clown any ideas about breaking bones ...
Too mumsy – riddle-y, not giggly.
NOPE!

She realised what she needed was a KID joke. Something to make Penny's knees buckle.

MEGA MIN-SPIRATION! She remembered! The sleepover where they caught Dennis's mum and dad having a secret fart battle!

Minnie ran an idea through her mind and smiled. Perfect. She raised her voice so everyone could hear . . .

'How do you know when a clown's pumped?' she shouted.

Penny stared back with her unsettling clown-frown.

Minnie paused before unleashing the perfect punchline: 'They smell FUNNY!'

She held her nose for full dramatic effect.

The joke and the way Minnie had told it, loud and proud, had a magical effect.

Penny doubled over giggling, her body shaking so hard with laughter that she dropped the ball and it rolled over to where Minnie was standing. Penny's laughter stopped. She was back to trying to be a scary clown again, but it didn't work. Minnie was no longer scared of clowns.

Clowns should be scared of Minnie.

This was her moment. There was only one move that would do it justice: the scorpion kick. She winked over at Whelan, where he stood holding one end of a 'We heart Minnie' banner, then prepared for the ultimate sting.

It was the single most epic moment of her life. The ball soared towards the top corner of the goal. Penny attempted to leap after it, but tripped over her own hilariously large feet. It went in.

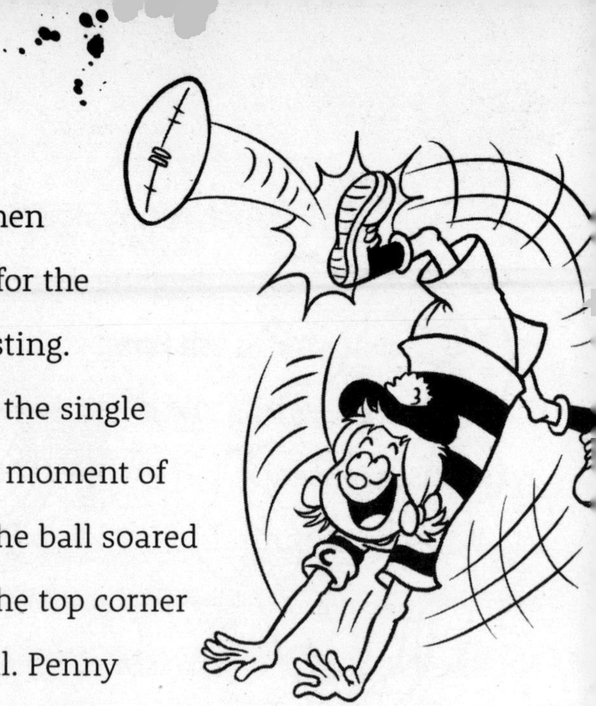

GOAL!

Penny rolled around on the ground, whining loudly.

'You must've broken your funny bone!' Minnie shouted. She guessed some of Dad's jokes were pretty amusing after all.

2-1 BASH STREET!

An ear-shattering cackle filled the air. Drusilla Kong was most amused!

It was the funniest thing she'd heard in several lifetimes. They'd done it. It was as if an ancient curse had been lifted. Even the Bogwarts supporters were smiling.

Medusa had returned to life, but hadn't got the memo about having a laugh.

'Things will be different the next time,' she hissed. But that's another story, for another day.

Bash Street had won. Minnie felt a huge wave of happiness wash over her before she was engulfed with congratulations.

Her mum, dad, brothers, Miss Mistry and Whelan raced to see who could hug her first.

Whelan crashed into everyone, as usual, creating a chaotic pile-up. No one cared. They just laughed. Everything was awesome.

Dennis hobbled onto the pitch. Minnie felt sorry for her cousin. He'd missed out on the action, for once. But Dennis was grinning from ear to ear. He was elated for his cousin. She deserved this win. He joined in the hug.

Minnie's parents both planted sloppy kisses on her cheeks. It was totally embarrassing, in front of all her friends, but she secretly enjoyed it.

Minnie realised the secret with families is to enjoy the Minnie-moments. It's only later on that you realise they've made your most mahoosive memories.

Minnie realised the life she'd always known had changed but, right here, right now she was Min-vincible! Nothing scared this girl anymore.

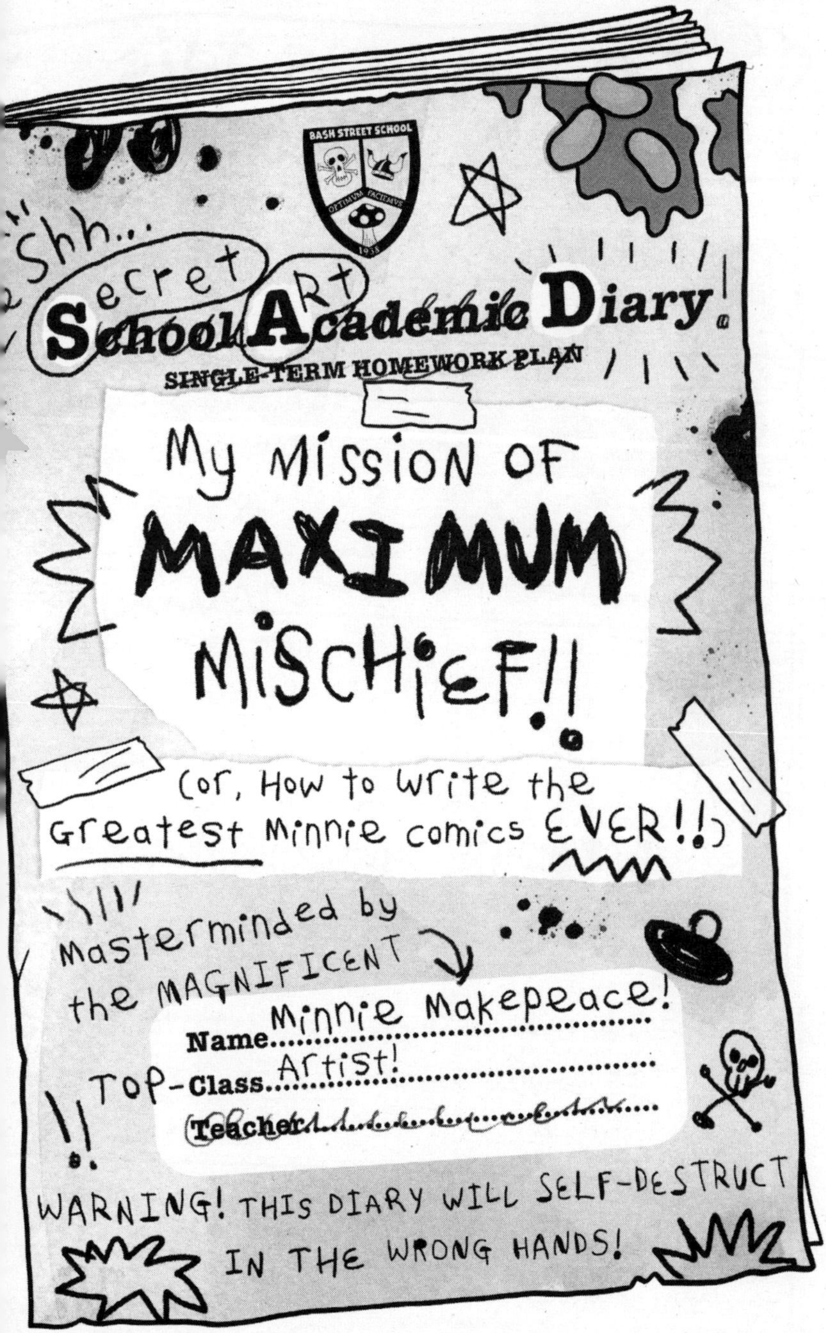

BASH STREET SCHOOL
OPTIMUM FACIEMUS
1938
Shh...
Secret School ART Academic Diary
SINGLE-TERM HOMEWORK PLAN
My MISSION OF
MAXIMUM
MISCHIEF!!
(or, How to write the Greatest Minnie comics EVER!!)
Masterminded by the MAGNIFICENT
Name Minnie Makepeace!
TOP-Class Artist!
Teacher
WARNING! THIS DIARY WILL SELF-DESTRUCT IN THE WRONG HANDS!

SO, WHAT'S THIS ALL ABOUT?

Good old (she's not old, really) Miss Mistry let me sneak a special treat into special copies of MY FIRST EVER BOOMIC!!

TEACHER OF THE YEAR

No, not my used gum from the cup final, but a world-class guide showing YOU how to start your own

* COMIC DIARY! *

A MIX of COMICS and a DIARY!

It's SO easy — even Dennis could do it!

LOL

Keeping one gets you used to looking for the funny stuff every day, and will help you understand your own life story.

PLUS, it 100% guarantees you'll always have something funny to read! — MINNIE!

MiNNiE CoMic RULES!

1. There are <u>NO RULES</u> really – just tips and tricks.

2. write for yourself first, before you think about sharing.

3. Your drawings don't have to be ~~perfec~~ perfect!

4. Draw <u>Fast</u> + <u>FREE</u>!

5. Mistakes are <u>NO BIG DEAL</u>! Just scribble it out and keep going.

6. Don't worry about missing a day.

7. It doesn't have to be 100% accurate!!!!

with a comic diary, you are creating a version of yourself that YOU control.

IT's YOUR STORY – YOUR RULES!

Tell it however you like!! You can even choose to draw things the way you WISHED they'd happened!!

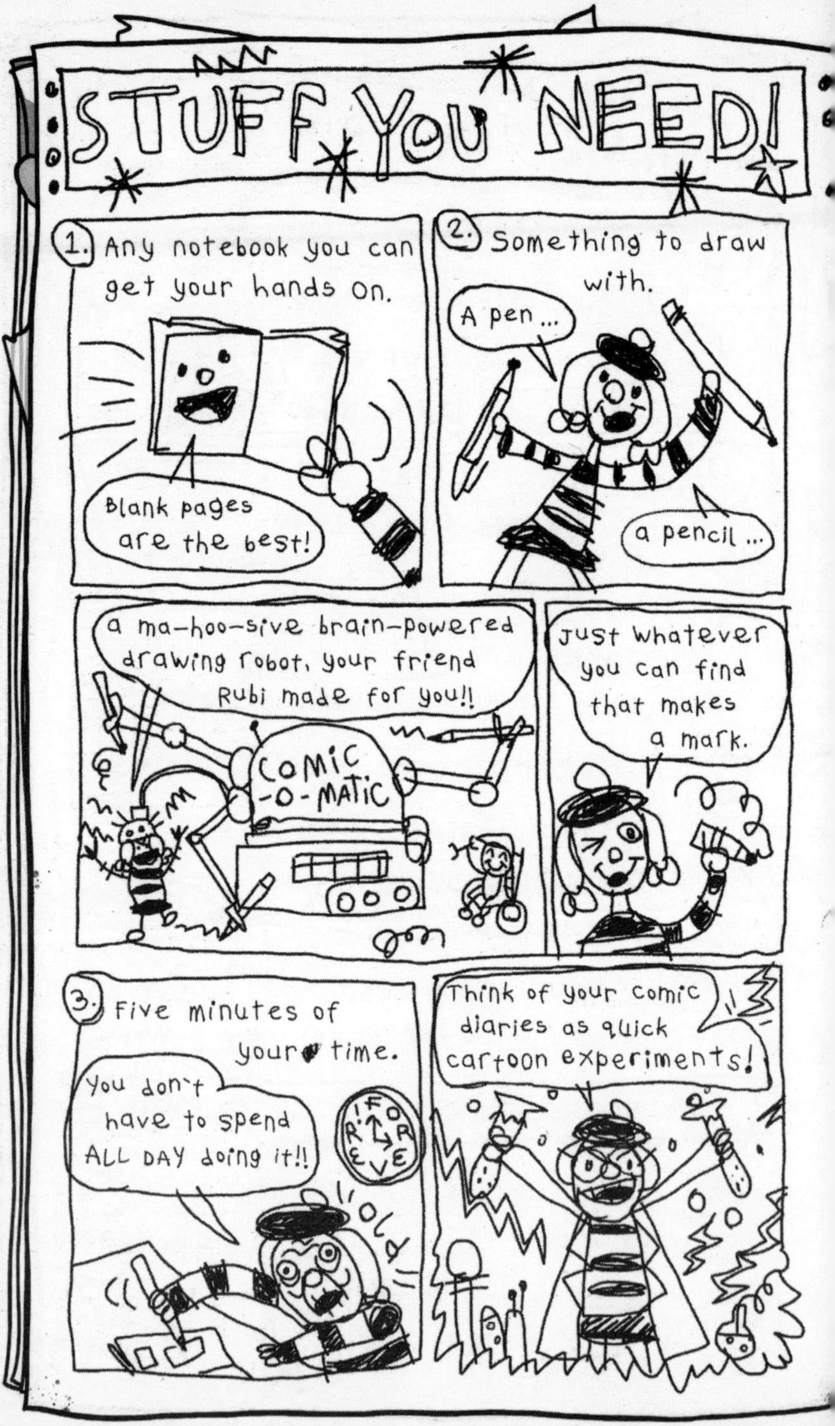
STUFF YOU NEED!
1. Any notebook you can get your hands on.
Blank pages are the best!
2. Something to draw with.
A pen...
a pencil...
a ma-hoo-sive brain-powered drawing robot, your friend Rubi made for you!!
COMIC-O-MATIC
Just whatever you can find that makes a mark.
3. Five minutes of your time.
You don't have to spend ALL DAY doing it!!
FOREVER
Think of your comic diaries as quick cartoon experiments!

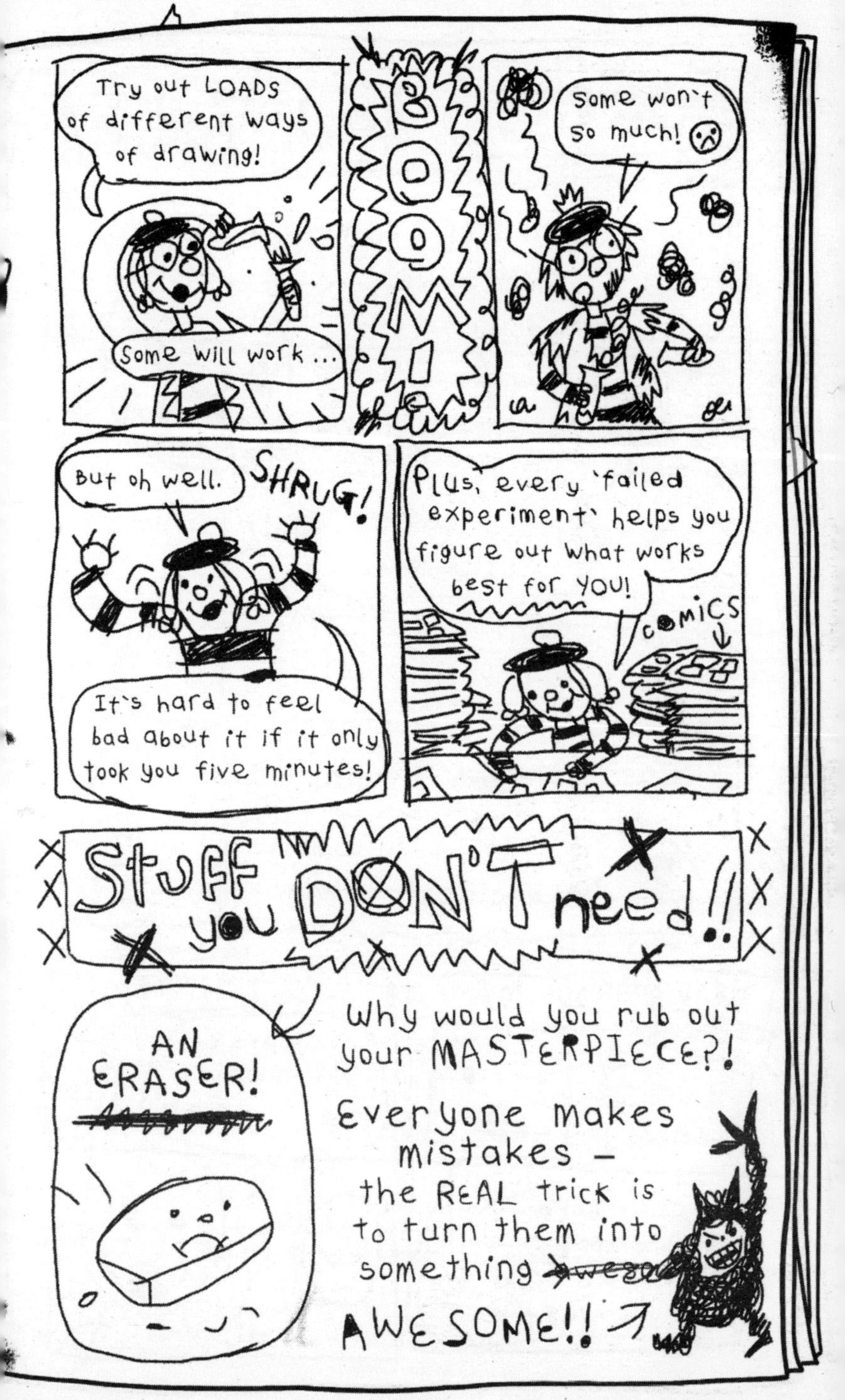

Try out LOADS of different ways of drawing!
Some will work ...
BOOM!
Some won't so much!
But oh well.
SHRUG!
It's hard to feel bad about it if it only took you five minutes!
Plus, every 'failed experiment' helps you figure out what works best for YOU!
COMICS
Stuff you DON'T need!!
AN ERASER!
Why would you rub out your MASTERPIECE?!
Everyone makes mistakes – the REAL trick is to turn them into something
AWESOME!!

Express Yourself!

Drawing yourself (+ your mates) might seem super complicated, but it can be as simple as drawing a stick-person.

HEY! I look NOTHING LIKE ME!!

... You might want to tweak the features for a better likeness ~~though~~ though!

Here are some of my classic Minnie moves:

HEAD SHAPE

Mum said I'd get square eyes from too much screen time — but this is RiDiCULOUS!

PiCK A NOSE!

Letters of the alphabet work really well.

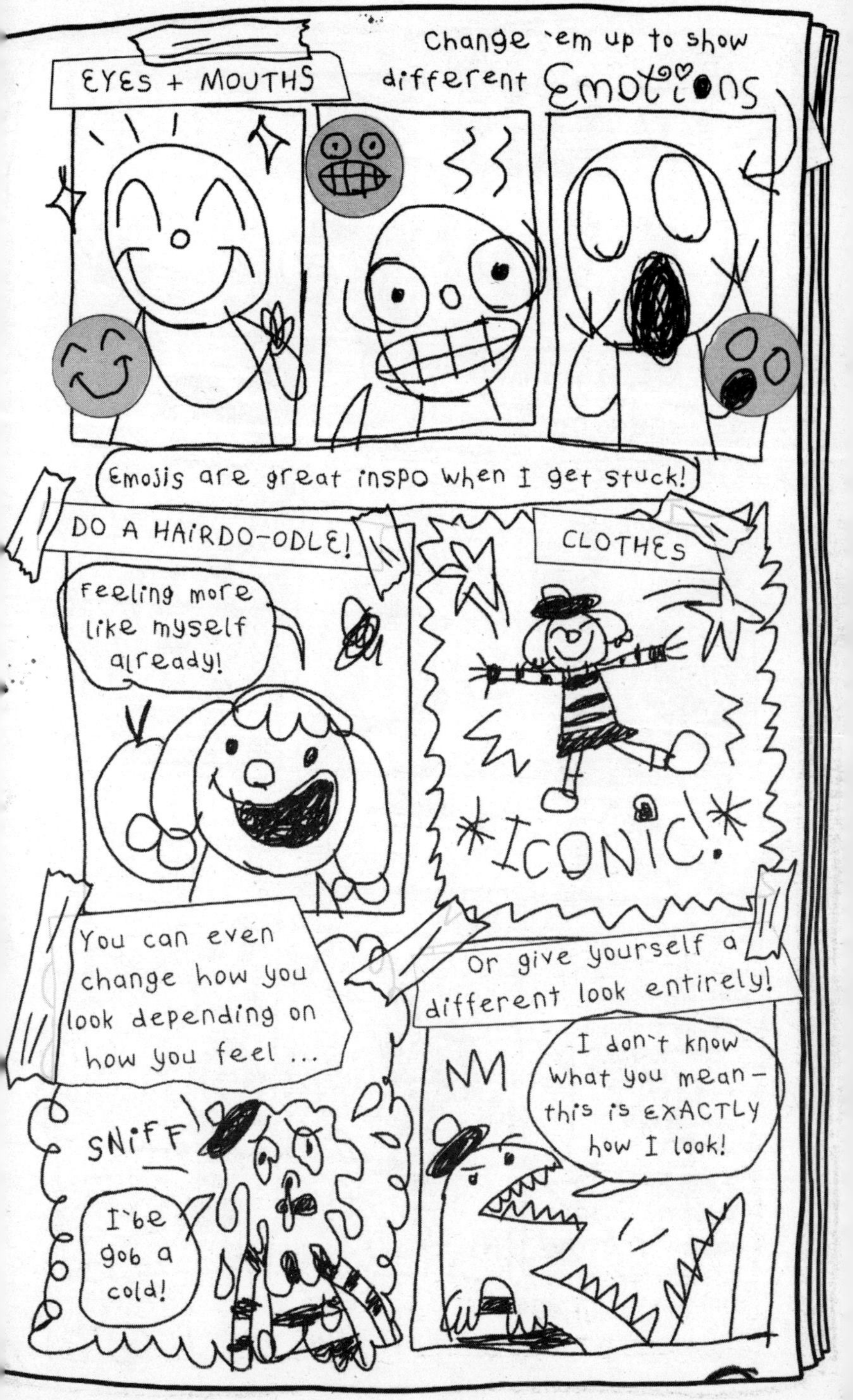
EYES + MOUTHS
Change 'em up to show different Emotions
Emojis are great inspo when I get stuck!
DO A HAIRDO-ODLE!
Feeling more like myself already!
CLOTHES
ICONIC!
You can even change how you look depending on how you feel ...
SNIFF
I'be gob a cold!
Or give yourself a different look entirely!
I don't know what you mean - this is EXACTLY how I look!

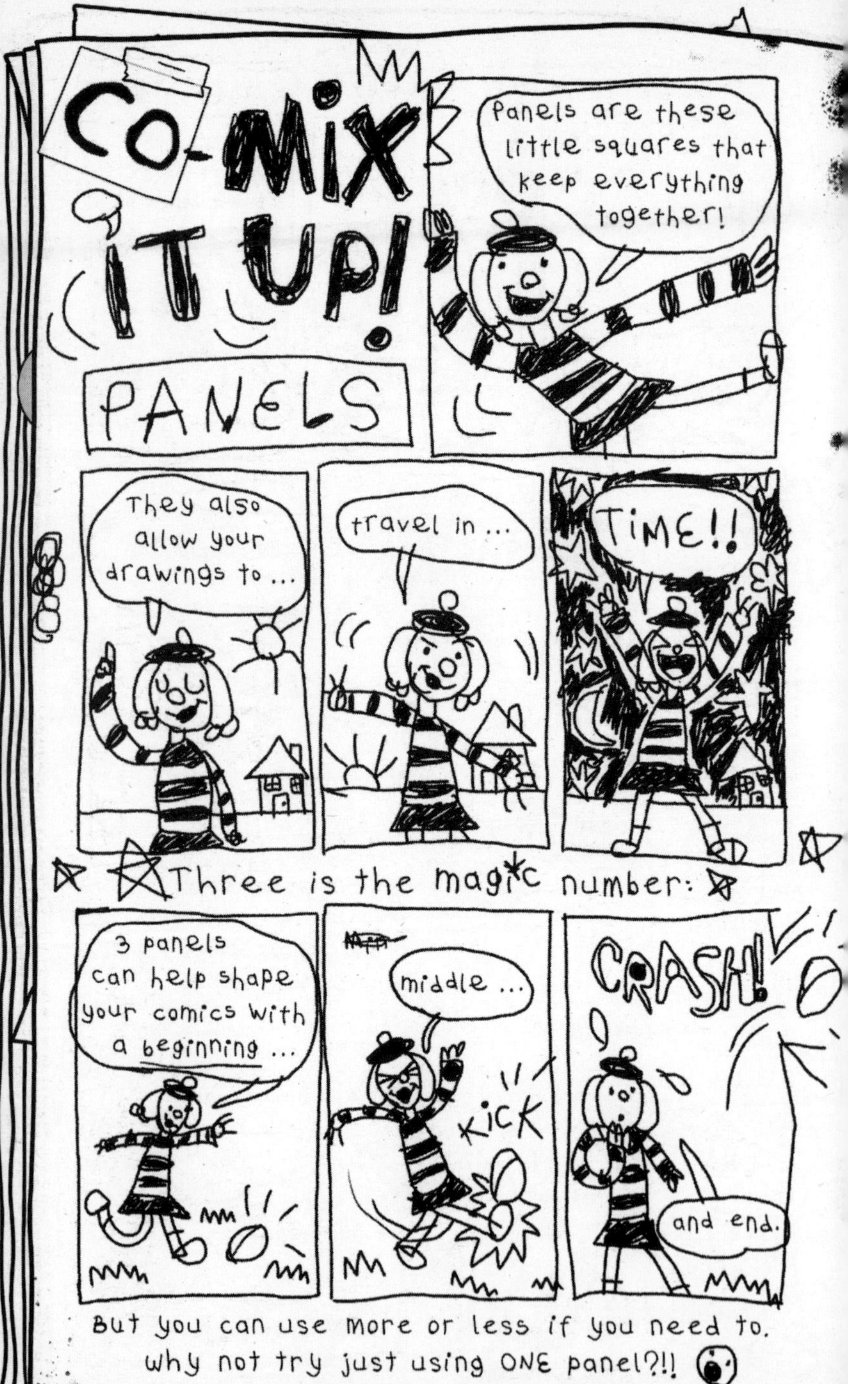
CO-MIX IT UP!
PANELS
Panels are these little squares that keep everything together!
They also allow your drawings to ...
travel in ...
TIME!!
Three is the magic number:
3 panels can help shape your comics with a beginning ...
middle ...
KICK
CRASH!
and end.
But you can use more or less if you need to.
why not try just using ONE panel?!!

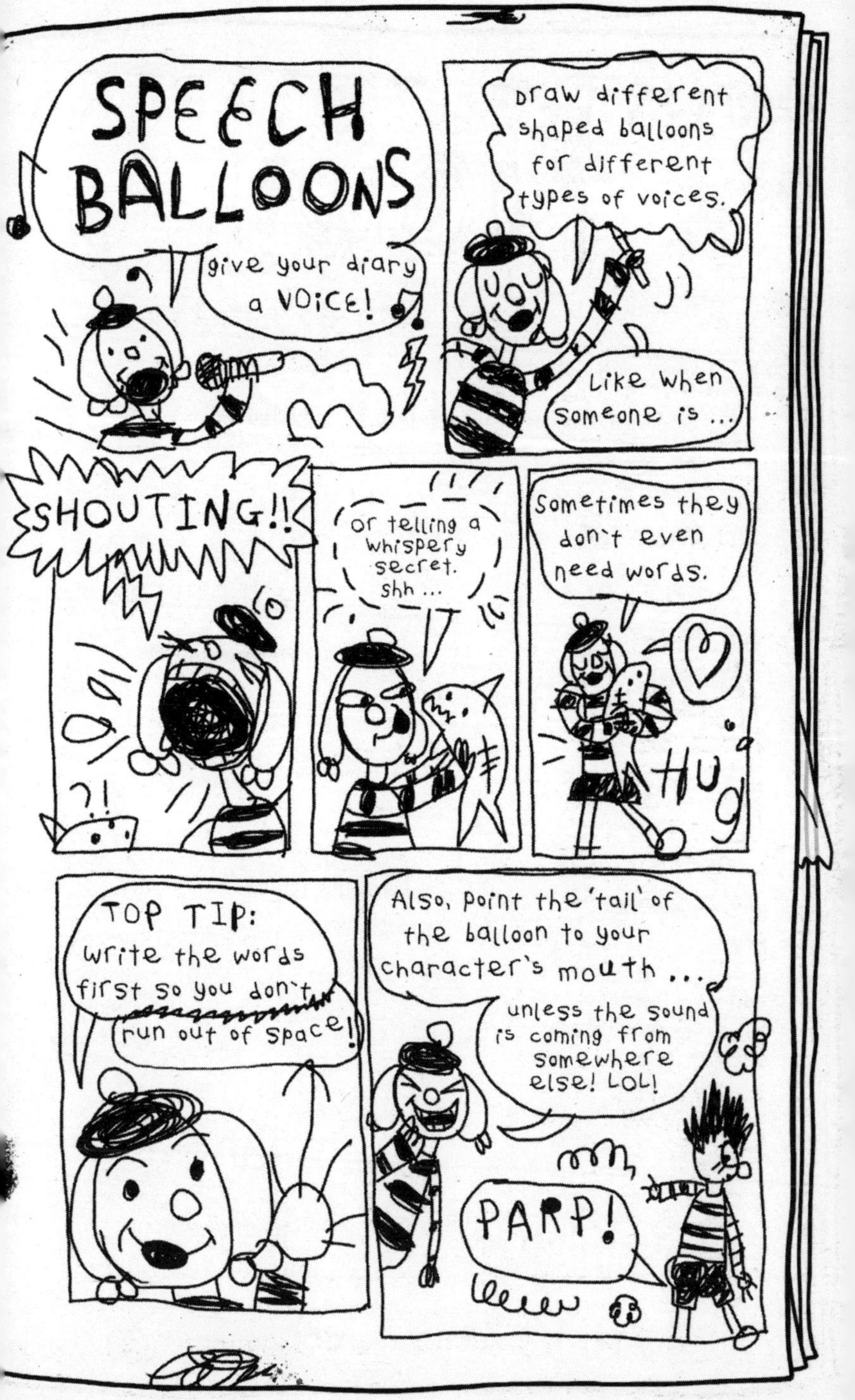
SPEECH BALLOONS
give your diary a VOICE!
Draw different shaped balloons for different types of voices.
Like when someone is ...
SHOUTING!!
?!
Or telling a whispery secret. shh ...
Sometimes they don't even need words.
HUG
TOP TIP: write the words first so you don't run out of space!
Also, point the 'tail' of the balloon to your character's mouth ...
unless the sound is coming from somewhere else! LOL!
PARP!

JUST GET STARTED
NOW!!!

Think about your day, today.
Pick a moment. Any moment.
Draw what happened. How you felt.

Some days turn out more special
than others. But keeping a comic
diary makes **every** day memorable.

REMEMBER: Just cos you're
inspired by something real,
doesn't mean you have to
KEEP IT REAL!!

Here's some MIN-spiration to
get you started:

- Something you did or saw
- The funniest moment of the day!
- An embarrassing moment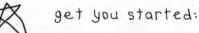
- A comic about something your pet did
- A weird dream you had!

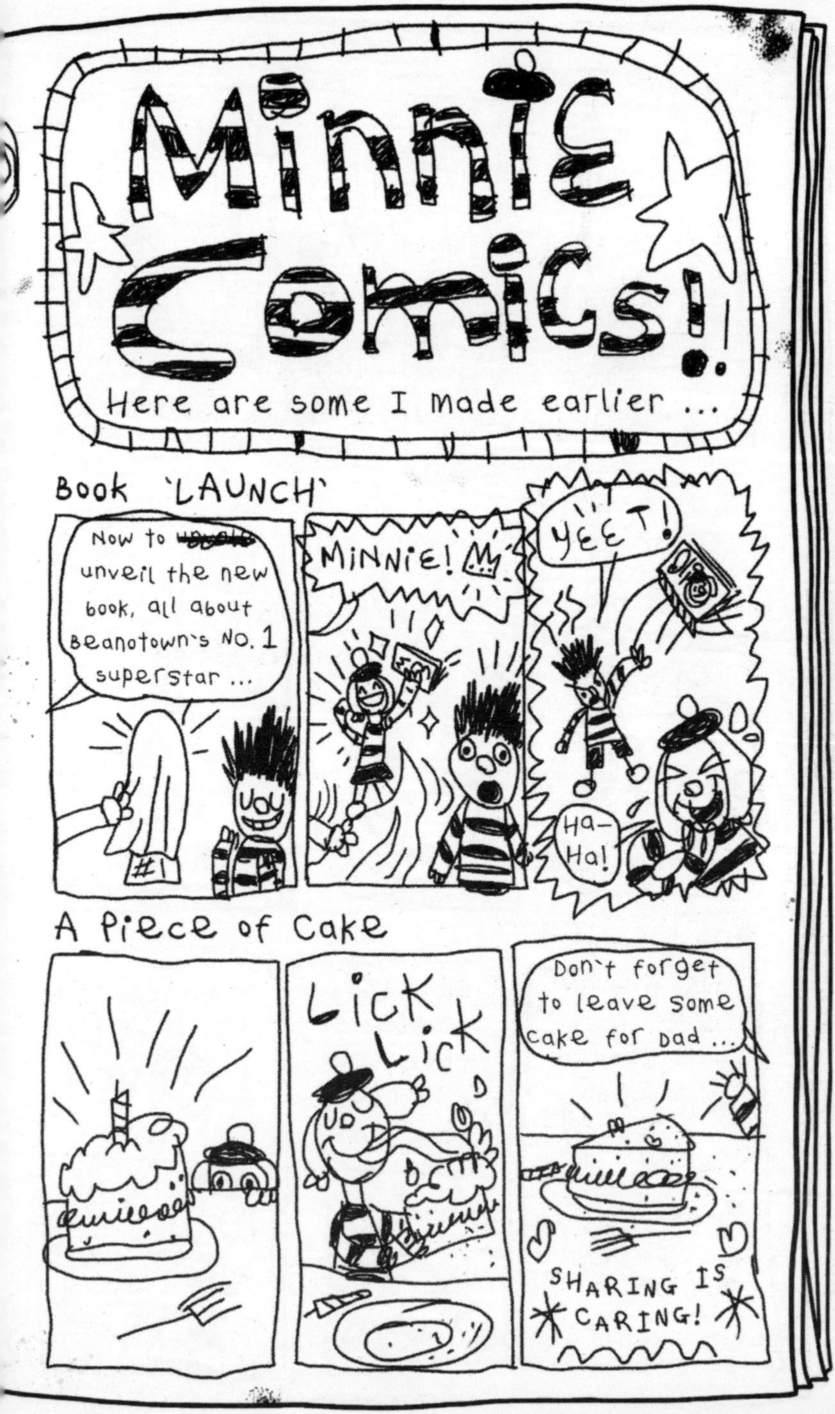
Minnie Comics!
Here are some I made earlier ...
Book 'LAUNCH'
Now to unveil the new book, all about Beanotown's No. 1 superstar ...
#1
MINNIE!
YEET!
Ha-Ha!
A Piece of Cake
Lick Lick
Don't forget to leave some cake for Dad ...
SHARING IS CARING!

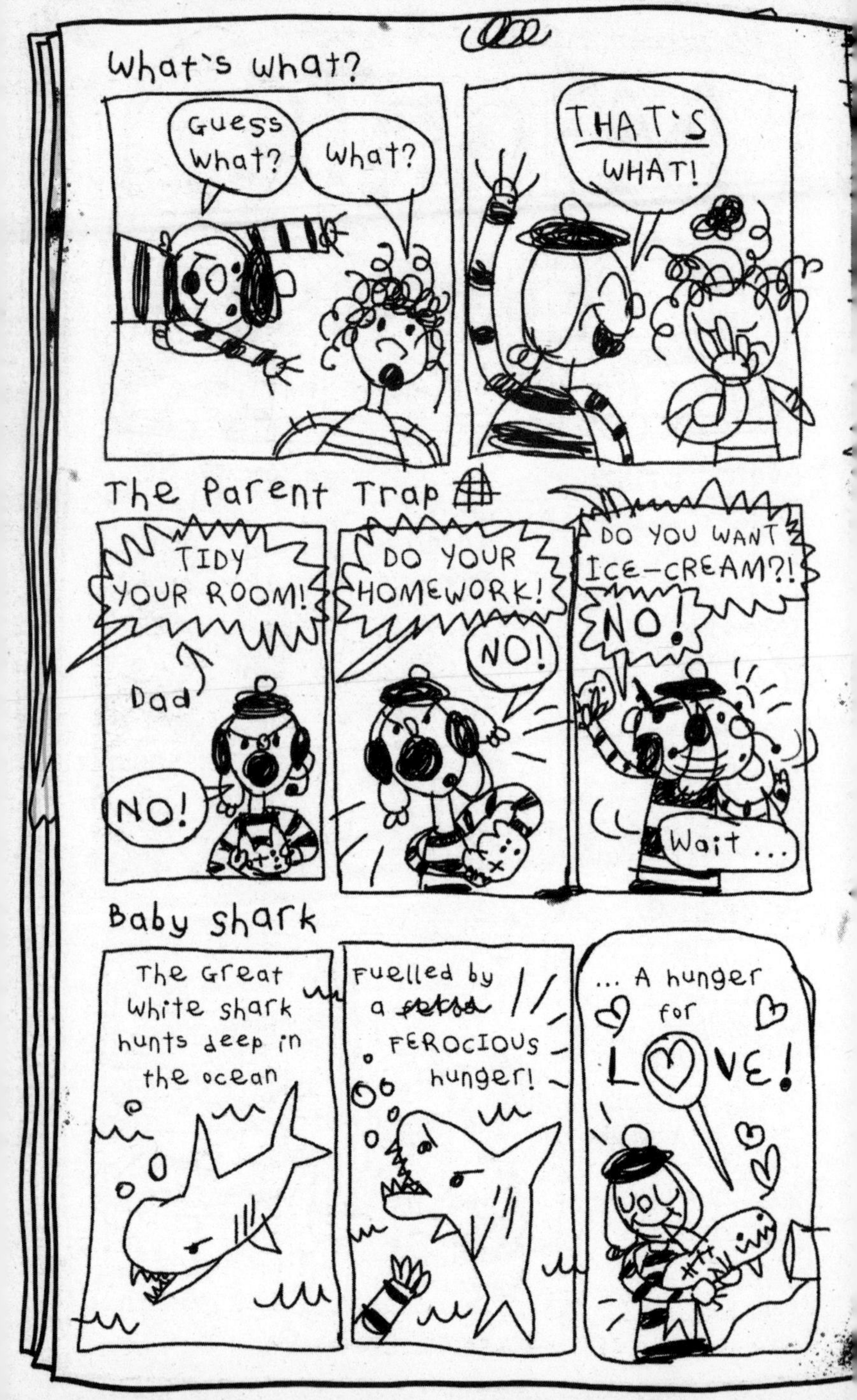
What's what?
Guess what?
What?
THAT'S WHAT!
The Parent Trap
TIDY YOUR ROOM!
Dad
NO!
DO YOUR HOMEWORK!
NO!
DO YOU WANT ICE-CREAM?!
NO!
Wait ...
Baby shark
The Great White shark hunts deep in the ocean
Fuelled by a FEROCIOUS hunger!
... A hunger for LOVE!

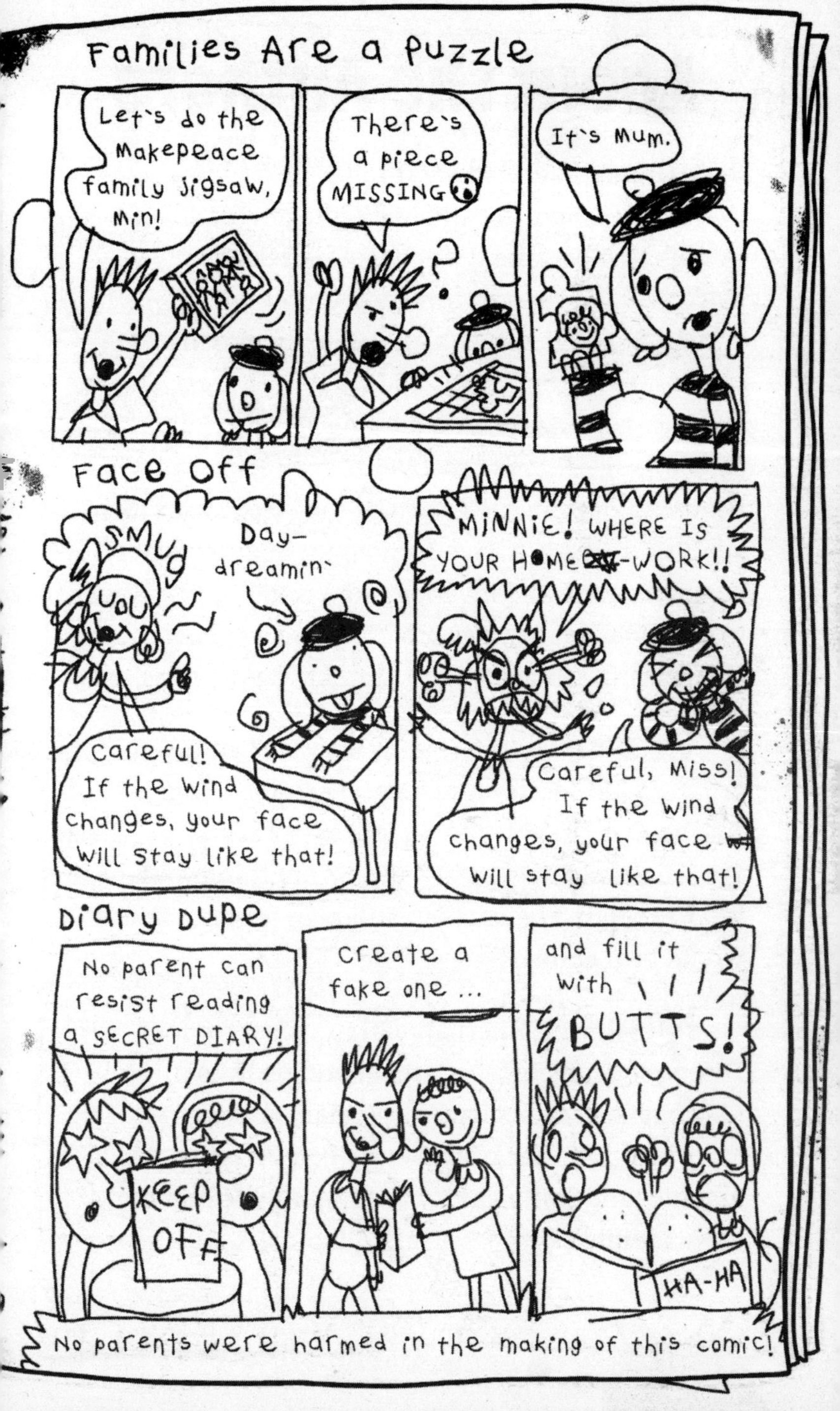
Families Are a Puzzle
Let's do the Makepeace family jigsaw, Min!
There's a piece MISSING
It's Mum.
Face Off
SMUG
Day-dreamin'
Careful! If the wind changes, your face will stay like that!
MINNIE! WHERE IS YOUR HOME-WORK!!
Careful, Miss! If the wind changes, your face will stay like that!
Diary Dupe
No parent can resist reading a SECRET DIARY!
KEEP OFF
Create a fake one ...
and fill it with BUTTS!
HA-HA
No parents were harmed in the making of this comic!

About the Authors

Craig Graham and Mike Stirling were both born in Kirkcaldy, Fife, in the same vintage year when Dennis first became the cover star of Beano. Ever since, they've been training to become the Brains Behind Beano Books (which is mostly making cool stuff for kids from words and funny pictures). They've both been Beano Editors, but now Craig is Editorial Director and Mike is Creative Director (ooh, fancy!) at Beano Studios. In the evenings they work with their genius Ed, Steph, at the Beanotown Boomix factory, experimenting and inventing new and exciting ways to let more kids than ever before discover how much fun reading can be! It's the ultimate Beano mission!

Craig lives in Fife with his wife Laura and amazing kids, Daisy and Jude. He studied English so this book is smarter than it looks (just like him). Craig is partially sighted, so he bumps into things quite a lot. He couldn't be happier, although fewer bruises would be a bonus.

Mike is an International Ambassador for Dundee (where Beano started!) and he lives in Carnoustie, famous for its legendary golf course. Mike has only ever played crazy golf. At home, Mike and his wife Sam relax by untangling the hair of their adorable kids, Jessie and Elliott.

IT'S YOUR FIRST DAY AT BASH STREET SCHOOL AND THERE'S SOMETHING STRANGE GOING ON.

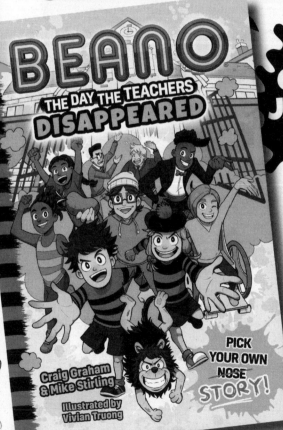

COMING JANUARY 2024

FOR EVEN MORE FUN HEAD TO BEANO.COM

JOIN THE KIDS OF CLASS 3C, AND DISCOVER WHAT IT'S LIKE TO BECOME A BASH STREET KID. IN THIS STORY, YOU RULE!

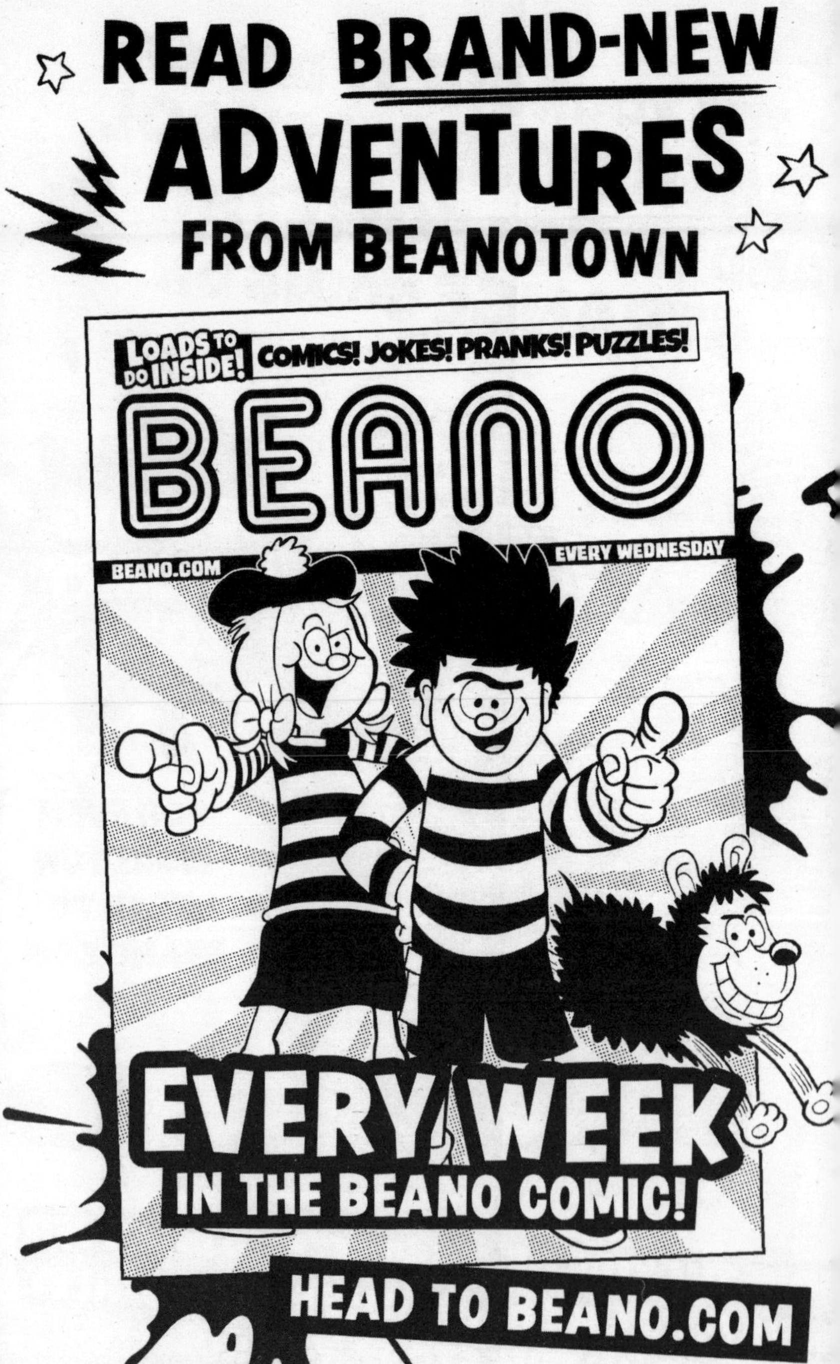
READ BRAND-NEW
ADVENTURES
FROM BEANOTOWN
LOADS TO DO INSIDE!
COMICS! JOKES! PRANKS! PUZZLES!
BEANO
BEANO.COM
EVERY WEDNESDAY
EVERY WEEK
IN THE BEANO COMIC!
HEAD TO BEANO.COM